Praise for Deborah Bedford and her novels

"Deborah Bedford grabs the reader by the heart and doesn't let go."
—*New York Times* bestselling author Debbie Macomber

"Deborah Bedford...will inspire readers with [a] message of hope and healing through the power of love."
—*CBA Marketplace* on *Blessing*

"From beginning to end Bedford... calls upon every emotion imaginable."
—*Christian Reading* on *Blessing*

"Both heartwarming and melancholy, Bedford's...poignant tale will find a home in all collections."
—*Library Journal* on *A Rose by the Door*

"[A] well-told tale that should appeal to readers of faith who enjoy an inspirational love story wrapped around deeper issues."
—*Publishers Weekly* on *When You Believe*

Dear Reader,

This book was originally published under the title *A Distant Promise.* The story holds special significance to me because it is based on my grandfather's farm in Waxahachie, Texas, and on the pecan grove where I loved to climb trees and gather pecans when I was a little girl.

This was the second book I ever wrote; now I've written almost twenty! I had to laugh when I began to go over it and found that I had attempted to write a book with teenagers in it when I was scarcely more than a teenager myself! Ha!

Now that I have two grown children, I found I was able to make a great difference in this story. I had a wonderful time honing the characters and rewriting it, so that this time it is being published for the glory of the Heavenly Father.

I am indebted to Joan Marlow Golan and Krista Stroever at Steeple Hill Books, who have given me the opportunity to "redeem" this work for the Lord. I hope you enjoy reading this new version. Visit me on my Web site at www.deborahbedfordbooks.com, drop me a note and sign up to receive my newsletter. Know that I love to keep in touch, and, most of all, I love to pray for you.

In Him, all life and peace,

Only You

Refreshed version of *A DISTANT PROMISE*
revised by author.

Published by Steeple Hill Books™

STEEPLE HILL BOOKS

ISBN-13: 978-0-373-78584-1
ISBN-10: 0-373-78584-4

ONLY YOU

This is the revised text of the work, which was first published by Harlequin Enterprises Limited in 1986.

This edition published by arrangement with Steeple Hill Books.

www.SteepleHill.com

Printed in U.S.A.

You are

at first

my friend

leading

me

through today

with a stronger hand,

a greater faith,

than I could find myself—

Reaching

Stretching

Handing me

my

shining

distant Promise.

~Debbi Pigg Bedford

This is dedicated to Tommie Catherine and to Jeff and Avery, my mother and children, respectively, for all they have given me—a faith in myself and a purpose for living, my past and my future, the simple continuity brought forth in all God's promises.

Acknowledgments

Special acknowledgment and thanks to
Alice B. Uehling, known lovingly as Abu
to all her adopted children. It is she who, with the formation of her nonprofit company Mothers-In-Deed, turned mothering into
a full-charge, managerial, professional career
and liberated hundreds of women
back into their homes.

There are literally thousands of families
around the world indebted to her, to her work,
to her dedication to children.

And to Tinsley Spessard, who so thoughtfully writes such deep and provoking study questions. Thank you for allowing the Holy Spirit to use you.

Chapter One

It was late September in the blacklands of North Texas, one of those blatantly sunny days when autumn hung crisp and cool in the air, one of those breezy days that hinted of sweaters, hot apple cider and football games.

Emily Lattrell half walked, half ran north on Dallas Parkway. She was as sunny and bouncy as the day itself as she made her way toward the cedar-etched professional building that housed Petrie, Simms and Masterson, the advertising agency where she worked.

Emily had a round full face with large eyes the color of maple syrup. She smiled often, and the overall effect—her round transparent brown eyes, her tiny nose, her defined, almost heart-shaped lips—was that she looked somewhat like a doll.

She wore a silk dress today, striped in shades of taupe and cream and gray. She'd knotted a scarf around her hips. The strand of eggshell pearls around her neck had been a gift from her father on her birthday last June, and they were perfect for her, especially today, because they picked up a confident gleam in her eyes that hadn't been there very long.

Emily worked as an account executive and copywriter at Petrie, Simms and Masterson. She'd been busy all morning keeping appointments with clients. Arriving at the office, she walked to her desk, pitched her purse inside a drawer, checked her secretary's desk for messages and then peeked through the glass partition that separated the creative boardroom from the hallway. Her immediate supervisor, Lloyd Masterson, stood chatting with Tim Johnson, a photographer. When Emily's boss saw her, he motioned her to enter. She opened the door and slipped in quietly behind Tim as he was speaking.

"I don't see any problem shooting the full length of the train interior. I'll try using my wide-angle lenses. When it comes time to do the layouts we'll have lots to choose from."

"Just be sure you don't lose the proportions of

the train," Masterson cautioned as he glanced up at Emily and gave her a welcoming nod. "We can fill only half the rows with people, if need be. You can always shoot from halfway down the aisle."

Already, Emily shook her head in disagreement. They were discussing the DART account—the Dallas Area Rapid Transit—and Emily felt strongly about it. That was one of the hazards of working in the advertising industry. They sold their ideas. But Emily's ideas and her boss's ideas were not always the same. "The proportions of the space don't matter at all, Lloyd. It's going to be the people who count in this campaign, not the stylized photography." Emily respected Lloyd Masterson. He had taught her almost everything she knew when it came to practical, hands-on knowledge of the advertising industry. And she wasn't afraid to debate ideas with him.

"Too bad you didn't get here sooner." Lloyd flipped a pencil into the air and watched it land a good five inches to the left of the ashtray he had been aiming for. "I could have used you—" he paused to smile "—to stir Petrie and Simms up a bit. All our ideas were so cut-and-dried this morning. That always worries me."

Emily was pleased by his compliment. She had been Lloyd Masterson's protégée ever since her graduation from UT, and she knew she owed Lloyd more than she could ever repay. That was one reason she was becoming gutsy lately. She wanted all their campaigns to be perfect, brilliant in every detail. For years she had been content to conform to Lloyd Masterson's ideas. But she knew that she owed him more than conformity now. The two of them had turned into a marketing duo worth reckoning with.

Lloyd frowned at the photographer and waved one hand, pretending impatience. "Go ahead and break for lunch, Tim. I'll call you when we've gotten this thing figured out. At this rate—" he cast a knowing look at Emily "—it may be midnight next Tuesday before we can make any final decisions about the proportions of the train."

"Like I said," Tim replied patiently, "I can bring all the wide-angles I've got."

Emily grinned at Tim. He had never once raised his voice to remind them that he was the professional photographer in the group.

Tim shrugged his camera case onto his shoulder and let himself out of the room. It was long past lunchtime.

"Okay." Lloyd turned back to Emily after the door closed. "Why don't we spend a few minutes going over your ideas?" He had a twofold reason for the suggestion. He was eager to hear her ideas. They were usually good. But he also wanted to show Emily that he had confidence in her. She had come to him with a good bit of enthusiasm and an appropriate degree from a good university. But she hadn't had much more than that.

Lloyd hated to admit it, but he had almost not hired her. She had seemed so frightened, so timid, at first. Something about her had won him over, though, something he had seen in her eyes. He had looked at her and seen raw honesty and strength and something else that suggested she knew how to survive. So he had taken her on. And he had never regretted his decision.

It had taken time to help her build her confidence, but he had slowly, by asking her opinion, by giving her increasingly challenging clients and by disagreeing with her ideas. She was a talented woman, and her lack of faith in her talents had seemed strangely at variance with her abilities.

"Let's zero in on some of the important aspects of this campaign and see what you can come up with," Lloyd said, pulling his thoughts back to the present.

"Fine." Emily paced past him. "What's first?"

"The copy," he answered, "which has already been approved by the client."

Emily nodded.

Lloyd continued. "The headline will read, Things You Can Do on a Train You Can't Do Driving a Car."

"Lloyd," Emily said as she paced the room, "tell me what the primary goal is going to be for this campaign."

Lloyd checked his notes. "'To increase ridership on the Dallas Area Rapid Transit system by fifteen percent,'" he read aloud.

"And how is this approach going to accomplish that goal?" Emily smiled at him, and Lloyd realized too late that she was carefully leading him on. He admired her for it, though. It was an effective marketing tool that he had taught her, and she was using it against him well.

Lloyd picked up another pencil and began flipping it into the air. "It will accomplish the goal by helping potential riders think of new reasons why they should be riding the DART train instead of sitting in a line of stalled cars on Central Expressway."

"Texans aren't used to mass transit. They're much more comfortable behind the wheel of their own cars." Emily plopped a manila folder full of notes onto the table and it landed there with a victorious *thwack*. "We alter their thinking by depicting people on the DART…"

"By depicting how they can best benefit by the time saved riding every morning." Lloyd didn't let her complete her sentence. She was coming close to dangerous ground now, a spot where they didn't agree. And he already knew it. "We need a man working furiously on a personal computer, a secretary taking dictation from her boss, a woman journalist with a notepad..."

"But those people are boring," Emily reminded him. "They don't appeal to me."

"They will appeal to our target market. Businessmen and women are the people we want to influence here. We need to make them realize how valuable their morning transit time can be. I want them to see this ad and feel that they're wasting their time when they find themselves stalled in a traffic jam. I want each of them to feel a great stab of guilt because they aren't already accomplishing things. We're trying to appeal to a hardworking, conservative group of people here."

"How do you know those things will appeal to our market? Are you guessing?" Emily leaned over the table, placed her weight on her elbows and stared at Lloyd full in the face. "I'm a businesswoman, too. And I want to see something that sparks my imagination. I want to see something that makes me think, that inspires me, that makes me laugh. Every time I look at that ad, I want to see something new, something I haven't noticed before. I want it to make me consider riding the train for new reasons. Ad campaigns and public service announcements have been throwing all the old reasons at me for years now. I'm still driving my car to work and battling Central Expressway every morning."

"These new ideas," Lloyd began, chuckling good-naturedly. "What might they be?"

"Fun things." Emily ran her fingers through her hair. "Outrageous things. Risky things." She began to pace the room furiously now, the way Lloyd knew she did each time she became so entranced with an idea that she forgot herself. He toyed with the idea of flipping a pencil at her to break her stride, but he decided it would be too mean.

"I'd like to see a bride throwing a bouquet out of the window and waving goodbye to the bridal party. I'd like to see her groom sitting beside her on the seat and giving her a passionate kiss while his mother scowls disgustedly from the seat behind him and holds up something horribly important that he's forgetting to take on his honeymoon… like his toothbrush or his eyeglasses or his underwear."

Emily paused to take a breath and Lloyd opened

his mouth to say something, but he didn't get the chance. "I'd like to see a ten-year-old boy wearing a snorkel mask and fins just peeking over the back of one of the seats. He can be obviously impatient for DART to stop so he can get off and go swimming at the city pool. And I'd like to see a man in a jogging suit—"

It was Emily who didn't get to finish her sentence this time. She was so intent on brainstorming that she didn't notice the door swing open. A man had been standing outside the glass partition for quite some time now, listening to her. He didn't mean to be eavesdropping, but it had long since passed time for his luncheon appointment with Lloyd Masterson. Lloyd had seen him there and had motioned to him to step inside the room. The man had been holding the door open for a few minutes, entranced with Emily's ideas. He couldn't resist finishing just this one sentence for her.

"I'd like to see a man in a jogging suit standing on his head in the conductor's seat while he steers the train with his bare feet."

Emily wheeled around to face the stranger. At first she didn't know what to think of the interruption. But the man was smiling at Lloyd, so he obviously was supposed to be here. Emily decided to play along with him. She grinned. *What an ab-*

solutely absurd, wonderful idea. I should have thought of it myself. She could change the copy to read: Fighting Dallas Traffic Can Be As Frustrating As Standing on Your Head.

"I like it." Emily did her best to appear serious, and she was thrilled when she saw the worried look on Lloyd's face. "This idea opens up an infinite number of new possibilities. Of course, it might be hard to get the right angle on the photo. What do you think, Lloyd?"

Lloyd was relieved when she let a touch of sarcasm intentionally slip into her tone. For a moment he thought Emily might actually have been serious. She loved to pounce on new ideas. But he saw that this time she was only teasing him.

"I think," Lloyd said as he stood up from the office chair where he had been sitting, "you should meet Philip Manning. Excuse her, Philip." Lloyd turned to the man who still stood in the doorway. "She can be a real live wire at times."

Philip Manning just looked at Emily without saying anything. She saw a strange expression flit across his face—amusement, coupled with sadness. Emily was instantly sorry she had spoken so impulsively. He obviously wasn't used to spontaneity. As she stood there, embarrassed, he finally spoke. "I'm the Manning Commercial Real Estate and Investment account." He glanced back at Lloyd. "I hope you don't mind me barging in like this. I had no idea you and your staff were still in a creative session. Your secretary wasn't at her desk."

Lloyd glanced at his watch. "I lost track of the time."

"So I can see." Philip waved his arm in a casual gesture of dismissal and then glanced once more at Emily. "I enjoyed viewing one of your famous creative sessions. I can only hope that the two of you argue just as effectively when working on my proposals."

There was a pause in the conversation, and Emily knew she should have taken advantage of the moment to interject some dry, witty comment. But nothing appropriate came to mind. She could only look at the man who stood before her. Philip Manning. There was something powerful about him, as if he had been born to be in charge of things. Although he was about six feet tall, physically he did not seem like a large man. But Emily knew of the stature he held in the business community. Perhaps because of that, he seemed to fill the room as she stood watching him. The company he had conceived and had coaxed into success, Manning

Commercial Real Estate and Investment, Inc., was one of Lloyd's most prestigious accounts.

His eyes caught hers and held her. At first they'd been clear, ice-blue, with a steely glint of confidence in them. But now there was something else in them, too. Something guarded. When Philip Manning looked at Emily, his eyes darkened.

Then, with no further ado, the man turned back to her employer. "Since we've missed our lunch, let's do our business here quickly. I need to get back," he said, glancing at his watch. "I have another appointment scheduled."

"I apologize, Philip." Lloyd glanced ruefully at Emily. He hoped he hadn't jeopardized one of his best accounts. Manning was a kind man, but he was demanding where his business interests were concerned.

Philip nodded in acceptance of the apology as he strode toward Lloyd. "I want to talk to you about the copywriting on this brochure, Lloyd." Emily had turned to leave the room, but she froze when she heard his words. He was holding up a brochure she had written. "I need to put together a portfolio about the person who wrote this."

"Is something wrong, Mr. Manning?" Emily asked. She was a relentless perfectionist when it came to the work she produced for the agency.

"Emily wrote the brochure, Philip," Lloyd explained.

Philip turned toward Emily. "I like your copy," he told her. He laid the brochure flat on the table beside her and pointed to the second paragraph. "Explain why you wrote this."

Emily glanced over her work and searched for an obvious answer to his question. He was pointing to a paragraph about the sales associates at Manning Real Estate. The copy said that his sales associates were seasoned professionals, that they benefited from and complemented one another because they sought to draw on one another's knowledge.

"That question is too broad for me to answer," Emily said as she turned to face him. "I'm not sure I understand what you want."

Philip laughed, a warm, kind laugh that belied the steel in his eyes, and leaned toward her. "I want to know why you used each specific word. I had thought you used a basic formula. But hearing that tirade about the DART ads, now I'm not so sure. Maybe you're a person who flies by the seat of your pants instead."

Emily thought for a moment before she commented. "There are several definite marketing techniques I used in this brochure. The things

Lloyd told me about your company showed me you place great stock in people. I had no choice but to use it as a marketing ploy. It is a very effective one."

Philip Manning studied her with approval. "I'm sponsoring a marketing seminar for my sales associates next week. There will be several specific workshops, many of which my own associates will be leading. At one of these workshops, I want to introduce the marketing tools your agency has produced for Manning."

"That sounds interesting," Emily said.

"Good—" Philip grinned "—because I'd like you to be there."

Emily's voice faltered. What did he want her there for? "I'm certain I could learn quite a bit."

"You misunderstand." Philip couldn't hide his amusement. "I don't want you there to learn, Emily, I want you there to teach. Actually, I had in mind Lloyd leading the workshop and then quietly introducing his copywriter. But, after what I just heard, I'd like you to do the workshop yourself instead."

Emily couldn't speak for a moment. How could she explain the creative process responsible for the words she had chosen? Certainly, she could explain the marketing tactics she had used. But she chose words because she liked the way they sounded, the way they blended together to form a rhythm, a harmonious idea. How could she present marketing statistics about something she had created because it pleased her? On the other hand, Emily knew her work had impressed Philip Manning. And she *did* know how the brochure should be presented.

As Philip Manning and Lloyd went on to discuss the aspects of a new project for the Manning account, Emily jotted several key words on a notepad. Speaking at the seminar would be an exciting challenge. It also scared her to death. She wanted to refuse, but there was something about Philip Manning, something about the trust he had already placed in her, that made her want to comply. The way he had sensed the small subtleties in her choice of words for the brochure, the way he approved of her writing, made her want to take a risk for him. And it made her want to risk something for herself.

Emily sat beside both of them for a while, in silence, while they talked. And then, finally, when the two of them turned their attention back to her, she nodded. "Okay," she answered somberly. "I'll do it."

"Are you certain?" Philip was concerned. He had seen her hesitation and it had surprised him. He had meant the invitation to be something of a compliment. He hadn't meant to put her on the spot. He touched her just lightly on the elbow, to reassure her. And when she answered him, she was thinking it was strange that here he was, so successful and certain what he wanted, yet still so kind and down-to-earth.

"Yes," she told him quietly, looking into his intense ice-blue eyes. They darkened once more as she gave him a determined smile. Emily wondered if she would ever have the chance to find out what caused this man's sudden somber expression.

Chapter Two

As far as Philip could see along southbound Central Expressway, there were lines of Suburbans and Beamers and Escalades, all of them reflecting the fierce Texas afternoon sun.

It occurred to him as he gazed on down the endless rows of fenders that he should have taken the DART train. Not even the carpool lane was moving. Philip smiled to himself. He was one of those conservative businessmen Lloyd and Emily had been discussing. And when he thought of Lloyd and Emily, his mind traveled immediately to the marketing seminar next week. He still had a hundred loose ends to tie up for the two-day workshop. One more guest speaker. Extra folding chairs for the front meeting room. The podium for Dr. Larsen's opening presentation Wednesday morning.

Philip needed to make a list for his assistant. Things always looked manageable to Philip when he wrote them down as lists. Lists made him feel as if he was totally in control. And he hated to admit how much he liked that feeling.

There were several things Philip had taken control of this week, several things he was extremely pleased with. Emily Lattrell was one of them. There was something about her that drew him to her.

Emily was a beautiful girl with an impish grin, flouncy bobbed blond hair and huge dark eyes. If Philip had seen her walking past him on the street, he definitely would have glanced in her direction. But he was thankful he had met her at Petrie, Simms and Masterson. He sensed something unusual about Emily Lattrell, a hint of sadness she kept hidden behind all that energy, some touch of vulnerability that caught him off guard. Philip had walked into Lloyd Masterson's boardroom and felt as if Lloyd had introduced him to an unbridled pony. Beneath all of Emily's bluster, he sensed an emptiness he had to admit he couldn't put his finger on. What could a girl like Emily be hiding?

As Philip drove south of Dallas on the freeway

and mentally surveyed the seminar checklist, traffic around him dispersed. At long last, he was out of the city. *Breathing room,* he thought. *Thank you, Father, that there's a place in this world where I can slow down.*

He had taken this route so many times now that he didn't need to watch the scenery. He could name the landmarks with his eyes shut. The Brookshire Inn. The Country Store and the Shell gas station. The turnoff to his brother's farm on the right. He took it, and seven minutes later he pulled in across the front cattle guard. As the car stopped in the gravel driveway beside the clapboard house, Philip could tell that nothing had changed. Everything about this place was subdued, now that his sister-in-law, Amanda, was gone. Everything was quiet and closed, as if life on the farm was slowly grinding to a halt.

Nine months ago, Philip recalled, the lace curtains in every window had been flung open so everyone inside could enjoy the fiery sunset across the Texas blacklands. And the sunset was just one of the things about country living that Amanda Manning had held dear. He remembered her talking about the meadowlarks warbling across the pasture. She took joy in the grapes that grew wild on the rickety arbor his brother, Clint, had constructed the year they'd married. She babied the geraniums she kept in pots on the second-story balcony that ran the length of the porch beneath it.

"Uncle Philip!" a boy's voice called from the front porch and Philip strode forward to greet his nephew, Greg. Philip hated to admit it to anyone, but of all three of Amanda and Clint's children, fifteen-year-old Greg was his favorite. Greg had been his firstborn nephew, and he was the closest thing to a son that Philip would ever know.

Philip was thirty-eight years old, almost thirty-nine, and he was beginning to believe maybe God didn't intend for him to ever have a family himself. He had opened himself up once to that kind of love a long, long time ago. And even though Philip was a forgiving man, this one particular wound still festered inside him.

Every time Philip did his best to put the past behind him, something would happen to remind him that his heart hadn't healed, and there he would be, wishing he could forget. So he had long since decided to remain married to his real estate investment firm, which made Philip Manning love the people closest to him, his younger brother, Clint, and Amanda and the kids, all the more.

Philip carried so many memories of them all, from long ago, before Amanda's operation, before things had become so incredibly complicated. He would never forget the October when Greg was six, when Amanda and Clint had gathered the family together to announce that there was going to be a new baby soon. Four-year-old Lisa had been excited and adorable, but it had been Greg who had made the day extra special, proudly displaying his knowledge of where babies come from.

"That new baby is in Mommy's tummy," he'd told everyone assuredly, and then he had marched over to Amanda, climbed into her lap and put his ear against her abdomen.

Just then, Amanda's stomach had growled, and she'd looked up sheepishly.

Greg had been overjoyed. "I can hear the baby!" he had shrieked. "I can hear the baby in Mom's stomach, and it's in there driving a car."

Driving a car still seemed like one of the most exciting things in the world to Greg. Philip wasn't surprised now to see him holding up two hands covered with axle grease. "Dad and the girls are inside. I'd hug you, but I don't think you want this stuff all over your good suit coat."

"Very perceptive, kid." Philip grinned. "I'll take that hug later, though, after you've scrubbed those hands. What vehicle are you operating on this evening?"

"The Studebaker." Greg nodded in the direction of the wooden garage that doubled as a storage shed. "I'm putting in a new steering column. I keep finding ball bearings all over the floor, and I don't have any idea where they're coming from."

Philip chuckled. "Sounds like you could use a good auto mechanic."

"I could," Greg called back over his shoulder as he started across the yard toward the garage.

Philip stood for a moment and watched Greg walk away before he pushed open the screen door and went inside. The front room was dark and empty, but from somewhere upstairs he could hear a pop song blasting. At least Lisa was home.

"Where is everybody?"

"We're in the kitchen," Philip heard his brother call back. "We're washing dishes."

When Philip entered the room, Clint turned to him immediately. It took a moment for his younger niece, Bethany, to do the same. Bethany had been born with a hearing defect in both ears. No one had known anything was wrong until she was almost a year old and her pediatrician had become concerned because she wasn't trying to imitate sounds. Clint and Amanda had worked with her deafness ever since then, and she had gone to a special school where she had learned to sign with her hands and then to read lips. By the time she was in the third grade, her teachers had decided to channel her back into the mainstream of public schools. She had caught up so quickly that even the kids in her class hadn't realized she couldn't hear. She was nine now, and she could read lips and understand almost every word that was being said. And when she saw her uncle in the kitchen, she ran and hugged him.

Philip had grown accustomed to speaking slowly whenever Bethany was in the room. He didn't really need to do that anymore for her, but it had become a habit. Even now, if there was ever a big word he wasn't certain she knew how to spell, he would bend down beside her and lovingly take her in one arm and sign it for her. "Hey, kid," he greeted her as he bent beside her. "Jumping Jehoshaphat," he said, signing the words. He had taught her how to spell *Jehoshaphat* when he'd visited the week before. "You're growing. Aren't you twenty years old yet?"

"Nope," she said as he squeezed her to him. It was a silly question but one that, in a complicated way, was appropriate for Bethany. She had taken it upon herself to become the little mother in this family. During the months that had passed since Amanda's operation, Bethany had seemed to take on the burden of an entire household. Now it seemed to take immense effort to get her to laugh. She planned meals and washed dishes and acted thirty-five, and both her father and Philip were worried about her. It was a rotten deal, a little girl taking over the job of a homemaker.

"Did you see Amanda today?" Philip asked his brother somberly. *Amanda. That doesn't even seem like her real name,* Philip thought. But it was what the family called her now. Clint had taken to calling her Manderly as he had grown to love her. It had been a term of endearment and it had suited her. The name echoed her spirit, her laughter and the silly nonsense songs she had loved to sing to the children when they were young.

Clint had not called her Manderly since her operation eight months ago. The name was for someone as vivacious as his sister-in-law had once been. It scarcely seemed suitable for the woman who lay in a coma in room 307 in the W. C. Tenery Community Hospital.

Amanda had gone to the hospital one morning to have minor surgery. And the surgery had been successful. But Amanda's physicians hadn't been able to stop the bleeding afterward, and her body had gone into shock almost immediately—despite the seventeen units of blood they had given her.

Since Amanda had fallen into a coma, the temporary childcare she had arranged and the three days' worth of dinners she had left for Clint to microwave had become permanent. She wasn't coming home. And so she became Amanda to everyone in the family again. Not their mother, Manderly. Clint had had to sit down and sign the spelling of Amanda to Bethany, who cried almost as hard as her father.

"I see her every day. A nurse lets me in before visiting hours every morning. That way I can read to her before I come home, get the kids up and start working." Clint reached out to Bethany and pulled her to him. Since his wife had been gone, he'd become very demonstrative with his children. As if holding on to each of them could show them how hard he was trying to hold the family together.

"Is she responding to sounds at all?" Philip's voice was gentle. He didn't know how much he should say in front of Bethany. He did know that she was strong, too. They had all been.

"Yes," Clint said firmly. This morning he had been reading to her, and she had flinched. It was a small movement in her right arm, and the doctor suggested it was an unconscious reflex. "I have to take that as a positive sign. I have no other choice. She's coming back to us, maybe tomorrow, maybe a dozen years from now after the kids have graduated from college. I know God answers prayers, Philip. He wouldn't take a mother away from three kids who still need her. He wouldn't take her away from me."

You can't always think that God is going to make everything turn out right, brother. I found that out a long time ago.

Philip was concerned about his brother. Clint looked even more exhausted now, more gaunt and gray, than he had looked just after Amanda's ordeal had begun. Philip hugged Bethany once again and took the dish towel from her. "You're a great kid, Bethany." He glanced pointedly at his brother. "I'm glad somebody's around to take care of your dad. He gets this crazy idea sometimes that he has to carry the whole world on his shoulders. By the way, where's your sister?"

"She's upstairs." Bethany set a glass in the dish drainer. "She's mad."

"She isn't mad at all of us," Clint reassured his daughter as he placed a stack of plates in the cabinet. "She's only mad at me. She's sulking up there." Clint turned to Philip and smiled with regret. "She's trying to make me feel guilty for something I refuse to feel guilty about—acknowledging the small but very pertinent fact that, yes, at thirteen years of age, she's still a child."

Philip laughed. "I keep forgetting how much I knew about the world when I was that age. What is it she knows more about than you do?"

"The junior-high field trip to Austin. Two classes are going by bus to tour the capitol building, then they're spending the night out camping. I think she's too young to go off on a trip like that."

"*We* went on a trip to the capitol about that time, Clint. Don't you remember?"

"It's the camping I'm worried about. You can't be too careful with a girl that age. I might consider it if I could go along as a chaperone. But I just can't get away from the other kids and leave Amanda that long."

"I can see your point with that." Then he changed the subject. "How's work coming?" Philip and his brother had the same instinctive feel for finances, properties and investments. They had inherited their talents from their father, Bryce Manning, who had been a successful stockbroker in Houston for many years before his death. Philip was thrilled to see his brother becoming successful. At a time in Philip's life when pursuing his own career had been a driving force, he had watched while Clint compromised to fit in with Amanda's family. Amanda, his brother's beloved

Manderly, had wanted to live away from the city, and Clint had agreed, after a month of indecision, to move his real estate company to Amanda's family pecan farm near Waxahachie. Living in the country the way he did, Clint could not maintain the cronies, the networking contacts, so important to a flourishing real estate career. He had made himself satisfied with the subdued career of a residential broker in a quaint Texas town known for its antique-shop-lined main street and its world-famous fruitcakes. For years all of Clint's listings had been farm acreages and Depression-era houses lined with gingerbread trim.

But as the boundaries of Dallas slowly edged southward, they brought with them an entirely new class of clients for Clint's Waxahachie firm. Since the advent of the Internet and the attacks of 9/11, people from all over the country had decided to move away from the urban frazzle of hordes of people, traffic and skyscrapers. Young professionals had begun moving to Waxahachie in droves, and they were purchasing the properties indicative of their flourishing careers. Clint was selling huge acreages with executive homes, tennis courts and swimming pools. It was success Clint had deserved for a long time. And because of Amanda's illness, the timing was a blessing. He kept a storefront office downtown, but he did most of his work from his study at home. That way he was home for the children.

Philip felt some sort of intense need to help his brother, to give him strength, to sustain him as he put his life back together. "You've done well," he commented as he watched Clint thumbing through an album of real estate listing photographs. "I'm glad you have something else to hang on to besides the possibility that Amanda might wake up tomorrow. Your work, at least, you have some control over."

Clint studied his brother's face. "It sounds like *you're* the one who's losing hope." Philip ran his life the same way he ran his business. Everything was written down in lists in indelible ink. "It isn't easy."

"I don't mean to lose hope in Amanda's recovery." Philip's voice was low. And then he changed the subject a second time. "So tell me about Lisa. What else is going on with your middle kid?"

"I wish I knew." Clint shook his head. "She scares me. She's like this miniature Amanda that is sometimes a woman and sometimes a dumb little kid. She's furious with me most of the time, and when I try to find out what's wrong she plugs in her earphones and turns on her iPod. A definite defense against telling anyone what her true thoughts might be." Clint leaned his head back and looked blankly at the ceiling. Then suddenly he winked at his brother. "I don't mean to give you the wrong impression. Me and the kids, hey, we're doing fine."

"I thought so." Philip was grinning now, too. Clint's good humor would help him present this new idea. "That's why I brought you this. Don't get mad," he added too quickly. "It's just a suggestion." Philip pulled a brochure from his jacket pocket and dropped it on the desk beside Clint's papers. If Clint agreed to try this it might take some of the pressure off where the kids were concerned. "The lady who runs this business rented office space from me today. We got to talking while she was signing her lease. I told her about you and the kids, and she suggested I pass her information along."

"What is this?" Clint unfolded the brochure. "'Absolutely Moms'?" He couldn't have been more bewildered. "Sounds like this lady has an interesting idea. But, Philip, why are you showing this to me? Bethany might benefit from it, but I doubt seriously that my two teenagers need a nanny service."

"Just read about it," Philip urged. "This is not a nanny service. What could it hurt to try? Many of these women are career professionals who opt for a life taking care of children, in a very nontraditional way."

Clint frowned. "This sounds wacko to me, brother."

"These ladies are well educated—some of them even have Ph.D.'s. They feel called as Christians to offer this service. They join the family and act like adopted mothers for as long as you need them."

Philip had been worrying about how to introduce this idea to Clint ever since Abbie Carson had signed her lease contract. Abbie's company was a national one, even international, but she was just opening her Dallas offices. And everywhere, her ideas had met with tremendous success. "These women come to your house as actual substitute mothers. They delegate chores, drive carpools, offer advice, give hugs and help with homework. And they bake brownies."

"You can buy brownies at a bakery."

Philip knew the idea sounded far-fetched, but he had a feeling about this. He had a feeling his brother might be ready to break under the pressure of being a caretaker. Call it a Holy-Spirit nudge, call it whatever you like, but Philip couldn't help feeling he'd stumbled on something that might help his brother. "These moms chaperone school field trips. They cheer at Little League baseball games. They spend time with one kid so you can spend time with another. You might even have time to get your hands greasy with your son out there on that Studebaker."

"You haven't signed us up for some reality show or something, have you? *Nanny 911* or some show like that? This family is falling apart, let's put it together while everyone watches."

"Maybe you need this," Philip stated drily.

"Nothing is going to put this family back together except for Amanda. She's my wife."

Philip had known this discussion might get difficult. "You owe it to yourself and to the kids to have someone take responsibility for this household. The kids would get used to having someone around the house again. Think about it, if Amanda *does* come home soon, you don't want her to find this place in total shambles, do you?"

Clint kept staring at the ceiling, looking skeptical.

Now, thought Philip, *I'm getting somewhere.* "Call this lady," he said. "I'll bet she matches you up with some spunky gray-haired grandma who turns all four of your lives upside down."

"That's what I *don't* want. Our lives have been turned upside down enough." But there was a strange conspiratorial acceptance on Clint's face, as if he wanted to tell his brother an interesting secret. "Do you think if I called this lady, this Abbie Carson, she might find an Absolutely Mom who knows how to pick out—" Clint lowered his voice further "—bras?"

Philip raised his eyebrows. And then he lowered his voice, too. "Don't tell me! Why do you need to know that?"

"It's Bethany," Clint confided. "I knew something was wrong the other day, but she wouldn't tell me what it was. Finally I got it out of her. She'd been changing clothes at a friend's house and the friend told her she was starting to need a bra."

"Oh, *no.*"

"She finally admitted how it embarrassed her. She finally got brave enough to ask if I'd go shopping with her. Let me tell you, I'm out of my league."

"I can't help you there, buddy. Can't she just go to the store with her friends and try that stuff on?" Philip was just as bewildered about those feminine things as his brother was.

"I don't think so." Clint shook his head seriously. "You have to talk to the saleslady and get measured and decide whether you're a B or an A or an F or something." He rolled a pencil across the surface of his mahogany desk in defeat.

Philip waved the Absolutely Moms brochure

in Clint's face. "You had better call Abbie Carson. Soon."

"Maybe I will." Clint retrieved the brochure from his brother's hand. "Maybe I will."

And this time, when Philip hugged his brother and the two of them stepped back and chuckled, Philip thought how much he loved them all. Amanda was everything to Clint, but Clint and the kids were everything to Philip. After all his real estate deals and his successes were said and done, these people and this place were the only things he had to hang on to.

Chapter Three

Five days later, as Emily Lattrell made her presentation at the Manning Commercial Real Estate Seminar, her metamorphosis took place just as Philip had predicted it would. Emily forgot about the podium, the people and the applause. It was as if she was in a creative session again, pacing around the stage at the front of the room because she was too exhilarated to stand still. She let her ideas emerge and take shape willy-nilly, and the wonderful part of it was that her ideas were good ones, effective ones. The faces in the audience melded together to form one face, one smiling new friend. Then, when Emily turned to make her way down the stage steps to rounds of applause, Lloyd rushed up to the stage and stopped her and handed her an award that she didn't even know she had won.

And after she was finished, people she didn't know kept grasping her hand, introducing themselves and complimenting her on the presentation and her writing and her award. It was a heady experience. And as Emily made her way through the milling people and the shaking hands, it occurred to her she ought to find Philip Manning and thank him.

As Emily searched for Philip in the crowd, she knew she owed her success on this day to her father. Her father had taught her to be persistent. As Emily had grown up, she had watched her father make a success out of the United National Bank of Decatur. She had watched him do it by offering much more than just the most contemporary banking services in the small North Texas town. She had seen him come out of his office to greet Mrs. Sliegner when she was making a twenty-dollar deposit into her husband's savings account. He would have treated someone making a $20,000 deposit exactly the same way.

When United National had to deny a loan to an applicant, Emily's father made an appointment with the applicant and explained why. And since he had been involved in banking long before automatic teller days, he had made certain each of his tellers kept a basket of lollipops and a box of dog treats to distribute to children and dogs respectively when a customer came to make a withdrawal. Martin Lattrell had made it his business to believe in people and have fun doing it.

It had been Emily's mother who had been so habitually untrusting. Two or three times a week, she would remind Martin of how fallible he was. "I had tea with Marge Fletcher at the club this afternoon," Emily had heard her tell her father one evening. "Marge says your bank loaned money for the Bridger project. I can't believe you would speculate like that, Martin. John got turned down by three major banks before he came to you."

Emily's father did lose some money in business dealings, but his faith in others had never dealt his bank the fatal financial blow that his wife was certain would come. Instead, the citizens of Decatur kept his bank alive with their twenty-dollar deposits, and finally, twelve years after United National had been chartered, Martin Lattrell had awakened one morning to find that he was an overnight success. The bank had flourished into an establishment with well over $63 million in assets. He had been featured in a small article on page fifteen in the *Wall Street Journal.* And the citizens of Decatur had elected him to serve as president of the Decatur Chamber of Commerce. He had done it. And he had achieved his ambitions strictly by caring about people. He hadn't even neglected the people he cared for in his own family.

The only thing that had suffered in the creation of Martin's success had been his relationship with Emily's mother. And United National had had nothing to do with that. Alcohol had done the damage; Emily's mother was an alcoholic.

At first Emily had been too young to understand her mother's violent mood swings. It had been like living with two people; one who was unhappy but loving, and one who was angry. Emily's mother would be gone from home for hours, and when she would return, Emily would lie awake for hours listening to her parents shouting. At times she was afraid to sleep for fear she would dream about her parents killing each other. And when Emily's younger brother, Jimmy, got old enough, he had the same nightmares. As she thought back over her childhood, the memories of those nights seemed to stretch on forever, Emily in her bare feet and her flannel nightgown sitting on Jimmy's bed, stroking his shoulders, telling him not to cry. And when Emily had grown older, she sometimes asked her mother why she shouted, why none of them could please her or why she'd broken the vase on the bookshelf. And Emily's mother hadn't remembered.

"That didn't happen, Emily," she would say firmly, her lips pursed. Her answers were stern and, now that Emily herself was an adult, she had to admit they were probably honest, too. She'd asked her mother so many times why she did this or why she did that, and her mother had no idea what she was talking about. She had been in a stupor. So Emily had learned to stay away. She'd learned to feel guilty for something she didn't understand. She blamed herself for her mother's unhappiness, thinking she had done something to cause it. And she blamed God for not answering her prayers and making her mother better.

It had almost been a relief when Emily returned home from the University of Texas on that first Christmas vacation from school to find that her parents were divorcing. Her mother was moving to an apartment in Fort Worth and entering an alcohol rehabilitation program. And Martin was going to do his best to get on with his own life. Emily dared to hope again.

But Emily's mother bounced from one alcohol program to another, and two years later, Emily began to face reality. Alcohol had drowned the very essence of a person who must have once loved her. And although she tried to rationalize her feelings, Emily felt as if in some way she was responsible. Perhaps if she'd been different, her mother could have confided in her or loved her more or... And even though she knew it wasn't logical, Emily felt she owed her father a debt that she could never repay. He had fought so hard to keep his family together all those years. But she still felt like a rudderless vessel, blown back and forth all her life by a force she didn't understand and had probably somehow invoked.

That was one reason Emily depended on her career. She needed the competition and the gratification, the reminder that she was worth something. Her career proved something to her—that she was okay, that she would survive. But no matter how hard she tried, the profit graphs and the plaques with her name on them couldn't chase away a faint grief and her feelings of not being good enough. She felt as if she had failed her mother somehow, at a time when it had counted the most for both of them—when she'd been a child. And that profound failure was something she couldn't talk about.

There was a hand-stitched baby quilt up in the attic that Emily's mother had sewn during the nine months when Emily had been on the way. It was covered with tiny brown cross-stitched teddy bears flopping and tumbling over their own heads. Below them, in the center of the quilt, Emily's mother had backstitched a poem she'd written in bright royal-blue letters:

Good night, sleep tight, my sweet baby bear.
The man on the moon keeps you in his care.
He embraces the night, beams a starlight smile
Beckons you to follow him a milky-way mile
On the back of moonbeams I once flew—
And now that journey I leave to you.

Emily didn't want any part of her mother's journey. Even so, there were times now when Emily would drive home to her father's house in Decatur, and when nobody knew it, she would pull the old quilt out and finger its stitches and wonder if her mother had loved her when she had stitched them. Then she would go with her father and sit beside him in the third-row pew at church on Sunday morning, even though she didn't believe that God was looking over her family. Even though she didn't believe that God answered prayer.

Why couldn't You have made things better between us, Lord? Why couldn't Mama have loved me enough to stop drinking?

Although Emily had gone to Sunday school

with her parents ever since she'd been a little girl, even though she'd once believed that, if she had faith in God, all things would work together for her good, her mother's ways had made her dubious. Emily's little-girl trust in Jesus had died during the dark times with her mom. The whole time everybody was singing and the preacher was giving his sermon, she would sit motionless, her slender fingers locked inside her father's firm strong ones, thinking she was just going through the motions for her dad, that she shouldn't be there. She didn't believe any of it. She couldn't stop thinking about a mother's love that she couldn't remember and trying hopelessly to understand where it had gone.

Emily had vowed she would never let anyone see the conflict she felt. She squelched it now as she searched the meeting room for Philip Manning. She found him standing in the doorway greeting his sales associates as they exited the room. People milled around him as he shook hands and nodded and looked satisfied. It was obvious to anyone watching that he was in command of this show. There was something magnetic about the man. Even a stranger at the seminar would have guessed he was someone important.

Emily waited in the crowd for a moment and watched him before she called out his name. He smiled at one of his associates, a broad, casual smile that produced tiny wrinkles at the corners of each eye. The lines on his face, the creases that ran from his nose around each corner of his mouth when his grin was at its widest, added definition and masculinity to Philip's already handsome face. His brown hair brushed back from his temples to reveal a hint of pepper-gray among the brown. Even the style of it, cut short in a precise curve around his ears and across the nape of his neck, made him look distinguished and larger than life to her.

Philip had a way of focusing on each person he spoke to, never diverting his eyes, as if the person in front of him was the only important thing in the room. Emily noticed his intense eyes, the way they flashed with light as he conversed with each of his employees.

Finally she called out to him. She plopped her notes on a folding chair with a determined smack and wove her way forward.

Philip's eyes locked with hers as she stepped toward him, smiling, carrying the gold plaque tucked beneath one arm. Her grin broadened as she approached him. "You're the one who got me into this." Her words sounded flippant, but her heart was beating so fast that she felt breathless. She was putting on a beautifully timed act for him, one that she had honed to perfection during the past years as an advertising executive. She didn't dare let him see past the perfect, poised mask she wore. "Thanks for the invitation to participate."

"I'm the one who should thank you, Emily Lattrell." He said her full name warmly. "This workshop was even more successful than I expected it to be." He nodded toward the plaque she was carrying. "And you obviously impressed members of the advertising federation, too. Congratulations."

"I'm always up for a challenge." She was smiling up at him as she spoke, and as he looked down at her, she reminded him of Clint's description of Lisa. She looked childlike—so dainty and small to him as she turned her face in his direction. But she was an adult who knew her craft and had just conducted a successful workshop. She was like Lisa, part little girl and part woman. And as he watched her, Philip felt a strange feeling of protectiveness building within him.

"Sometime next week I'll have my assistant bang out an official thank-you note," she said. "But since I'm here right now and feeling on top of the world, I thought I'd come over here and shake your hand in person."

Philip extended his hand to her, and when he

took her delicate fingers with the glossed nails into his own, he could already feel her pulling her hand away from him.

He wondered why she thought she needed to be so formal. She had certainly been more relaxed when they were laughing about snorkelers and brides and men in jogging suits riding the Dallas Area Rapid Transit. He decided to keep her talking just a little while longer. "How's the DART campaign coming along?"

"The same," she said with a hint of humor. "Lloyd and I are still in the 'compromising' phase." She shrugged, her eyes twinkling, and she reminded Philip of a little girl again. "We're the same place we were when you walked in on us the other day. Butting heads. But we're getting there."

"It's going to be interesting to see what you come up with once you and Lloyd finish hacking away at each other." Then Philip gazed down at her and grinned. And, just like that, he asked her to lunch. He didn't exactly know why. He just knew she seemed like a mystery to him, and he wanted to be with her a while longer. He didn't know when he would see her again. And just seeing the drollery in her eyes made him forget the pressures of his business and his worries about his brother.

"Thank you," Emily answered him softly. "I'd

like that." There was something about his invitation, something about the way he kept looking at her, that made it hard for her to turn away.

Emily waved goodbye to Lloyd and gathered her notes. Philip Manning motioned to her from the doorway and she followed him. He'd just stepped back and held the door open for Emily when a deep female voice called out his name from behind them.

Emily saw Philip's body tense. He turned and said coolly, "Hello, Morgan." His neutral facial expression revealed nothing. Emily couldn't read any emotion there.

"I stopped by to see you and I happened in on that dog-and-pony show instead. I'm impressed," she told Philip slowly. "Very impressed."

He reached out and steered Emily through the door. Emily sensed that he wanted to get as far away from the woman as possible, and the sooner, the better. "We were just leaving," he said as he gripped Emily's arm. "I'd like you to meet Emily—Emily Lattrell, this is Morgan Brockner, president of Brockner Associates." His eyes proved unreadable. "Morgan is my biggest competitor here in Dallas. Your presentation this morning was designed to give my company an edge over hers."

Morgan Brockner's name was just as familiar to Emily as Philip's had been. Lloyd had tried to get the Brockner account a long time ago, when her business had been smaller, before Philip Manning had offered them an agency retainer. Lloyd didn't believe in handling competing accounts.

"Hello, Morgan." Emily extended her palm to the woman. "It's nice to meet you."

"I enjoyed your little presentation, honey. It was quite—" Morgan glanced back at Philip "—interesting." Morgan did not take her hand.

"Thank you." Emily folded her arm behind her.

Morgan spoke to Philip now, and Emily felt invisible. "How is the Robertson deal coming along? You close on that two weeks from Wednesday, don't you?"

"Yes. We do." Emily didn't know Philip Manning well, but she sensed he was on his guard. He acted like Morgan Brockner had just mentioned a sale that was meant to be confidential. *Who was this woman to him?* Emily wondered.

As she watched the exchange between Philip Manning and Morgan Brockner, she couldn't help but notice his reaction as the two of them talked. He had seemed to literally harden, as if his face had turned to stone the moment the woman had called his name. Something venomous and sharp hung in the air between them.

Emily watched Philip try to escape. "I'm sure you'll excuse us, Morgan."

"Certainly." Morgan flashed Emily an almost imperceptible smile. "I didn't mean to detain you."

Emily and Philip walked to his car in silence, and Philip held the door for her as Emily slid into the front seat of his Audi. And as she studied the passing scenery, she sensed Philip was a million miles away.

Emily screwed up her courage. "I shouldn't ask, should I?" This was just a business lunch after all. "You want to tell me what all that was about?"

Philip stared ahead at the traffic in front of them. "That was about a woman who never leaves anything to chance. She isn't a person I can trust." His fingers opened on the steering wheel, closed again. "The sad part is, every time I see her, she seems to enjoy reminding me of it."

Clint and Manderly had shared so much richness, so much texture, in their lives together, Philip reflected as he drove. For him, there had been one woman a long, long time ago, who had made him think he could have that richness in his life, too. Morgan Brockner.

Once upon a time, he and Morgan had planned to share their businesses and their lives and live happily ever after. He had met her during his junior year at Texas A&M, in corporate management class. She had been everything then that she was now—polished, poised, treacherously beautiful. They had worked together on a group project for class and, one night, when the three other members of the group had left them to pick up a pizza at the all-night place down the street, Philip had told Morgan he'd like to date her.

Looking back on it now, Philip realized he should have seen the warning signals even as their relationship began. Morgan had never seemed to laugh or do anything silly. She'd been intensely serious about her future, so serious that they'd never discussed his future, only hers. When he wanted to talk about Clint and Manderly or his Sigma Chi brothers or his faith in God, Morgan wanted to talk about the investment firm she was going to build. And one day in class, she had simply passed him a note that said: "I think we ought to consider getting married someday."

Philip wasn't certain he loved Morgan. She was always there for him and very beautiful, and he was the envy of all his frat brothers when she waltzed into a room on his arm. But he didn't want to lead her on, and he wasn't certain his feelings for her could be classified as love. It all seemed so logical to him, the two of them together. Their relationship was something that had happened between them because of convenience and not because of passion or romance. She even seemed to share his faith. She went to church with him on Sundays, and that was important if they ever considered having children. And they had continued talking about building a business together as if they were talking about a marriage.

When the time came for them to march across the commencement platform with the other graduating business majors, Philip had decided to give committing himself a try. He wanted to see what it was like having Morgan as a partner. He would start by asking her to become a partner in the real-estate firm, and they could build it together. Maybe later they would be partners for life. His father had already agreed to finance the initial operation for him.

Morgan had accepted his offer on the spot. In fact, she hadn't seemed too terribly surprised. When she'd said yes, she had reminded him of an overzealous actress who had had her Oscar acceptance speech prepared for weeks. He realized later that he had hit upon the perfect analogy. An actress accepting an Oscar. He knew it now; that had been the day he had almost seen through her.

Five months later, when the company's first

major commercial deal had come through, Philip signed it over to Morgan. He had made the sale himself. The property consisted of three storefront offices near a shopping center, and the commission had been an amount that made his head reel. And Philip thought Morgan had been worried about money. He wasn't. He had his father's backing. He had enough capital to see him through three years at a loss, if need be.

But Morgan needed something to live on. She had been out beating the streets without much luck ever since the company started. Giving her this transaction was Philip's way of showing Morgan how he felt about their future together. He wanted to give them a chance. He left the contract on her desk with a note thanking her for sharing his successes. Thinking back on it now, Philip wondered if his note had been the last straw for her. Morgan had never wanted to share anyone's successes—she had wanted to devise her own.

The next morning when he had barged triumphantly into her office to see what she had to say to him, all her belongings had been moved out. He stood inside an empty office.

Morgan had run away with Philip's contract. For days, when he'd tried to call her, she hadn't answered her phone. And sometime during the next week when she had answered the phone, she had a new official title on her résumé. Morgan Brockner. Sole owner and president of Brockner Associates. Every penny of the commission he'd given her had gone to start a competing company.

For months Philip couldn't accept the fact that Morgan had seduced his trust, then betrayed it. But as days went by, Brockner Associates grew. Morgan Brockner had used him. Everything they had shared together—the hopes, the goals—had been a farce. Morgan had picked him out from corporate management class for her own use just as easily and as meticulously as she had pulled a dress-for-success outfit from her closet. Everything she did was a means to an end. *How could he have been so blind?*

It wasn't the fact that Morgan had betrayed their business partnership that still bothered Philip. It was the fact that she had betrayed his personal trust. He had opened himself up to her and had given her the very things that made him what he was—his dreams, his triumphs. When she left the office, Philip felt as if a part of him had been amputated.

She had fooled him for two and a half years. Even her faith had been false. He was never going to be fooled again. He had stumbled along, bitter, proud and sad, and he had survived by giving his soul to his company. It was ironic now. Morgan was probably the one major reason he had been so successful in building Manning Commercial Real Estate and Investment. He had decided to defeat her at her own game. He made certain that whenever the sales figures came in at the end of the fiscal year, Manning Commercial Real Estate and Investment was just a bit farther up the scale than Brockner Associates.

His goal was to be better than she was—always. And gradually the bitterness he felt toward Morgan had subsided and changed into a determination to keep Manning Real Estate on top. He had built it from the ground up in much the same way he would have raised a child.

And sometimes when he had trouble understanding Clint's deep pain and his fight to regain his wife, Philip would picture himself and pretend something terrible had happened to his company and he would wonder if, like Clint, he would find strength enough to struggle and survive.

Chapter Four

Three brochures for Absolutely Moms, Abbie Carson's company, lay on the dashboard of Philip Manning's car. During the man's long, silent reverie, Emily picked up one and leafed through it. He hadn't spoken to her once since they had left the marketing seminar after meeting Morgan Brockner. They drove on a bit farther while she read the brochure, and at last Philip glanced over at her. Emily smiled at him, and when she did, the hardness in his face softened a bit. He turned his gaze back to the road, and then he nodded toward the pamphlet she still held in her hand. "Did you read that? Abbie Carson has quite a business."

"Nice brochure," Emily commented. She was always looking at marketing pieces, analyzing them and getting ideas for her own work for clients. "Which company put this together for her?"

Philip glanced at her and grinned slightly, then once more he turned his attention back to the road. "Are your interests purely personal? Or might they be professional, as well?" he asked her pointedly.

Emily laughed. "Both, I suppose." She folded the brochure again. "I was just wondering what the competition is putting together these days. I'm always curious."

"That particular brochure was designed by a San Francisco agency. Abbie Carson keeps her corporate home office there. Abbie is going to be in Dallas for a while, though. She's opening a branch office. She leased office space from me in Stemmons Towers."

"Is that why you're carrying her brochures around?" Emily asked. "Or are you going to sign up to become an Absolutely Mom?" It was an outrageous thing to say just then, when she just barely knew him, but she was desperate to bring some of the life back into his eyes. She cocked her head and gazed at him. "Or is she trying to find someone to mother you?"

Finally he laughed. When he did, the tension lifted in the car. "Yeah," he answered. "That's it. I was thinking about signing up. To be a mom."

"You think you'd be a good one?" Emily asked, grinning.

"Abbie Carson is going to need someone to update that brochure for her Dallas market," Philip said. "I'll give her your name."

"Thanks." Emily was always grateful for new business contacts.

When Philip exited the highway, he glanced her way. He needed someone to talk to, someone to take his mind off his unsettling encounter with Morgan. Even if they had just joked about Absolutely Moms and talked about nothing important, their conversation proved a nice diversion. And then, when the light turned green, Philip decided to explain to her why he really had the brochure in his car.

There was something about Emily that seemed natural and soft, and he let himself feel drawn to her for a moment. He didn't know exactly what it was—maybe the fact she had remained silent most of the drive and hadn't attempted to force a conversation in the wake of his brooding. He sensed she was a good listener and a fair person. Quietly, with resolve, he began to tell Emily about his brother and the kids. He told her about Amanda and the farm and the tragic results of his sister-in-law's operation. And then he paused. "That's why

I'm trying to talk Clint into calling Abbie Carson. Those kids need someone, and so does he. And someday maybe they'll have their mother back."

Emily watched as he spoke about his brother's family, and she saw Philip's jaw sag. Something sadly vulnerable washed across his face, and the melancholy look in his eyes surprised her. She suppressed an urge to reach across the car and touch his shoulder. She was tremendously moved that he had decided to tell her about his family. There were times when she needed to tell someone about her family, too, but she simply couldn't. Her mother's alcoholism was something she kept hidden, something she shared with no one. And Emily found a strength in Philip, a strength that she didn't have, because he was able to talk about things that mattered to him.

"What happened the first time the children saw Amanda after she had gone into the coma?" she asked softly.

Philip was shaking his head. "Nothing. They haven't seen her. Clint won't let them."

"Why?"

"It's one of those things he can't let go of." Philip raked his fingers through his hair. "He wants the kids to think of Amanda the way she used to be. He doesn't want them to see her lying there looking frail and fragile. He's afraid they'll see her and begin to lose hope."

Emily stared out the window, letting her eyes follow the numerous skyscrapers as the car whizzed past them. "Kids have a knack for imagining things to be ten times worse than they are." She remembered her own nightmares all too clearly. Her parents hadn't murdered each other, after all. But there were times she still wondered how close they might have come.

A cell phone rang in Philip's pocket and he fished inside his suit jacket to find it. He glanced at the screen on his Treo and apologized to her. "It's my brother. I'm going to take it." There was a pause before he said, "Clint? What's up, bud?"

Emily watched as Philip's expression grew concerned. "No." Another pause. "That doesn't sound good. Where do you think she went?" Philip cast a sideways glance at Emily. "That does make sense, though. No, it's fine. I'll get someone to cover for me this afternoon." He stopped speaking for a moment and just listened and looked desolate. "It won't be the worst. We won't let it." He pressed the end button.

"Lisa's missing," he said. "Clint's middle kid. I'm sorry. I need to go out there. I need to take you back."

"Let me call Lloyd." Emily dug in her purse for her own cell phone. "Maybe you could just drop me off somewhere." Emily couldn't conceal her own worry. She had an important creative session scheduled for this afternoon. She hated to make Philip backtrack to North Dallas when he was anxious about his niece. And Emily was anxious about her, too. Philip had just spent fifteen minutes telling her about his brother and the children, and Emily felt as if she already knew them.

Lloyd answered on the second ring. "What's the status on the creative session this afternoon?" she asked.

"I'm glad you checked in," Lloyd said. "Our client canceled on us. He got called out of town unexpectedly. We've rescheduled for next Wednesday at three."

"Is there anything else you need from me this afternoon?"

"Are you trying to get out of an afternoon of work?"

"Of course I am. I'm a creative genius, Lloyd. We need our downtime."

She hung up the telephone, and Emily's voice turned serious as she made her offer. "You don't have to take me back to my car, Philip. Leave me off at a DART stop and I'll catch the train."

Emily hesitated, then finished it. "Or I could go with you."

Yes, it was a bold offer. But it was also honest, born of caring for a teenage girl she didn't know but who she guessed might feel very much the same as she once had felt. Emily had run away from home several times, too, because she knew her mother didn't want her. But she didn't dare tell Philip that. "Let me look for Lisa, too."

"We can use all the help we can get." And Philip fell silent as they drove past Oak Cliff, headed south into the country.

The North Texas blacklands spread out before them as Philip turned the car off the main highway and headed over the rise on Maypearl Road toward the farm. The Manning place was still a good three miles away when Philip pointed it out to her and Emily saw the homestead for the first time. It was backed up against the horizon, atop a hill, framed by the sheer richness of green and black patches of soil. Living here, Emily thought, one would be aware that there would always be another season to come, another harvest, another springtime.

"It's beautiful," Emily said.

"I know," Philip replied.

They both fell silent once more.

When Philip's car rattled across the front cattle

guard, and they pulled up in front of the house, a man strode toward them from the porch. After he'd quickly introduced Emily, Philip said, "We got here as fast as we could."

It surprised Emily how closely these brothers resembled each other. Clint was an earthier version of Philip. He was shorter and stockier, but his eyes were the same and his face creased in the same places.

"Lisa never showed up at school," Clint said. "They called to see if it was an excused absence. I told them she'd left for class at the same time as always. But by the time we talked, we figure she'd already been missing for three hours."

"Did you call the police?" Philip asked.

Clint nodded. "She can't be classified as missing until she's been gone a full day. A trooper did check down at the bus station and didn't find her, so unless she's hitchhiking—which I don't think Lisa would do—she's still in town. The guy at Greyhound promised to call if she showed up trying to buy a ticket."

"What was she wearing?" Philip asked. "Were you able to give a good description?"

When Clint nodded and repeated his report—jeans, black T-shirt, blond hair in a ponytail, pierced ears—Emily's heart sank. His description fit probably a third of the girls in the Metroplex.

Philip asked, "Does Lisa have a group of friends she hangs around with? Are there parents you could check with? Maybe a group of girls has gone off together."

"She used to have a group of four or five other girls, but that was months ago. I wouldn't even know who to call now. She just stays up in her room listening to her iPod music at top volume and we have our nightly quarrel. That's Lisa's social life."

"Your nightly quarrel last night," Philip said, "was about the school field trip to Austin. Am I right?"

Emily gazed across the rolling meadow that spanned the horizon behind the house. How clearly she remembered the desperation of yearning for a mother who might never be there for her again.

"Do you mind if we pray together before we start searching?" Clint asked as he reached a hand toward each of them. "Do you mind if we pray for her safety? And to help us find her quickly?"

"Of course we don't mind," Philip said. Then maybe he thought he'd overstepped his bounds in answering for both of them. He glanced at Emily with an apology in his eyes as if he'd suddenly realized he ought not to have spoken so quickly.

"It's fine," she reassured him. And she bowed her head as their fingers slipped together. For the first time in years, Emily lifted her heart to the heavens in supplication. For the first time in years, she lifted her heart to a God she'd relied on before her mother's deeds had set her straight. No matter how often she'd prayed as a child, she'd felt like her prayers had fallen on deaf ears.

"Only You, Father," Clint whispered. "You're the only one we can totally rely on. Show us who to go to to find Lisa. Show us where to look." Emily felt Clint's hand tightening around hers, he spoke so fervently. And in her other hand she felt Philip's palm clasping her fingers, warm and strong and reassuring. "Keep Lisa safe, Lord. Please. *Please* keep her safe. In Jesus' name we pray. Amen."

And, almost as soon as Emily lifted her head from the prayer, she remembered the places she used to go, the things she had once needed to do when she was almost overpowered by the circumstances life had dealt her. Emily wheeled toward Clint, a strange boldness overtaking her. "I'd be willing to guess that Lisa's on this farm somewhere. Does Lisa have a place she goes when she wants solitary time? A place that's away from the house?"

"Not that I know of."

"I used to hide in the alley behind a neighbor's garage," she volunteered, not realizing she'd broken a vow to herself not to speak of her childhood.

"It got to be too much sometimes. I needed to go off, to get some time alone."

"I want to check in town," Clint said. "I want to see if anyone's spotted her."

"We'll stay here," Philip suggested as he glanced at Emily beside him. Just this morning he had been comparing Emily to a child and thinking how much she resembled Lisa. Now here she was, standing beside him with her back set against the world. She seemed so sturdy, so strong to Philip just then, and he wondered why she was taking this search so personally. Finding Lisa was obviously very important to her.

"Do you want to change?" he said. "There's chiggers out there, and cow pies, and the stinging nettle will kill your legs. Clint wouldn't mind, and I'll bet Amanda's jeans would fit you."

"I don't want to take the time, Philip."

"In the long run, I think it might save us instead. If you've got on farm clothes, we'll be able to cut through the pastures."

After Philip found her something to wear, they searched the farm in the barn, the tack room and the corral. After they had no luck there, they combed the meadow and made a trek through the cow pasture. And as Emily walked along beside Philip making suggestions, she suddenly felt her heart well up into her throat and she was horrified; she thought she might cry again. It was as if seeing this family in such an upheaval had evoked emotions she hadn't let herself feel in years. Fear. Loneliness. Shame. And she couldn't explain it, but she was glad he had included her in this search instead of dropping her off at the DART stop on the way through town. "Philip." She said his name tentatively. It almost sounded like a question. She reached out and gingerly touched the crook of his arm. He stopped and turned toward her. "Thank you."

"For what?"

"For bringing me out here today." Emily wanted to find Lisa, but she felt like she was searching for something else, too. She felt like she'd come out here with Philip Manning and had started looking for herself, too.

She was thanking him for the conversation in the car about his family. She was thanking him for letting her glimpse a part of him that she doubted other people ever saw—his concern for his brother, his love for his family. It made the little gold plaque with her name on it that she had won today seem like a sorry excuse for a life. He had so much more than she did.

"We call this 'The Little Place,'" Philip said, interrupting Emily's thoughts as he pointed up a rutted road. The road, he explained, crossed fields that the Manning family leased out to a cotton farmer. Amanda's family had bought this property during the Depression after the house had burned to the ground and the tenants couldn't afford to rebuild it. "After Amanda and Clint took over the farm—" Philip held up a length of barbed wire so Emily could climb through the fence "—Amanda's father built a cabin in the pecan trees and kept a few cows grazing the property."

"What's up this way?" Emily asked, pointing in the other direction.

"Just the trash dump. Several fishing ponds the kids used to use. The burned-out foundation of the old house."

"This place stretches in every direction, doesn't it? I hadn't realized."

Philip pointed. "There's another small barn and a corral up that way, too. It has a hayloft. We should probably check it out."

"You go on ahead." Emily shaded her eyes and peered off in the opposite direction. "If it's okay with you, I'll have a look around the pecan grove."

"She won't be in the cabin, Emily." Philip gazed down at her. "That place has been locked up for years."

"I don't expect her to be in the house." Once more, Emily gazed back at the peaceful grove of trees. Something about it drew her. "There may be someplace else we've overlooked."

Philip left her then, and Emily was alone. From all around her came the early-evening trilling of the cicadas and the melodic call of the meadowlarks. As her legs swished through the tall grass, Emily felt alone in a world all her own. Inexplicable peace enveloped her. How Amanda's parents must have loved this place, she thought. They had loved it enough to pass it on to their daughter and, through her, to her children. How they must have enjoyed watching their grandchildren growing up strong and sturdy on the land.

Emily found herself wishing she had roots like this to share with children someday. Motherhood suddenly seemed not so intimidating to her. Peanut-butter-smeared cheeks, grass-stained knees, little fists full of this dirt. Emily closed her eyes and imagined herself and her own brood of children climbing the grape arbor and hanging upside down on the trellis.

That's when she suddenly sensed someone watching her. She heard a muffled sound from above in the leaves.

"Hello?" she called out as she gazed up into the leafy branches above her. She had a pretty good guess who might be above her in that pecan tree. A pecan fell at her feet. "Lisa? Is that you?"

No one answered, but as Emily watched, the limbs moved above her. The tree swayed and the leaves that had already started to turn from the frost began raining down on her. Another pecan hit Emily on the head as someone descended from a high perch. Emily waited quietly by the tree, and finally her patience paid off. First there came a pair of blue feet followed by jeans and a black T-shirt. Finally Emily caught a clear view of melancholy eyes, a pale, grieving face. The girl crouched in a fork just above the trunk of the tree. The sight of her took Emily's breath away. She looked so delicate, so fragile, and she reminded Emily of a little bird who might flutter away at any slight movement. "Lisa?"

As the girl nodded her answer, Emily thought she must be the most beautiful, tragic-looking teenager she had ever seen.

The two of them stared at each other. And it was Lisa who finally spoke first. "Yeah." Then, "Who are you?"

"I'm Emily." She shielded her eyes from the evening sun that was close to the horizon as she answered the girl's question. "An associate of your—" Emily hesitated, uncertain how she should classify him "—your uncle Philip's. I was with him when your father called. He wanted your uncle to help look for you. Everyone is concerned that you're missing."

"Missing?" Lisa pronounced the word as if it were foreign to her. "Has he been looking for me since lunch? How did he…?"

"You know junior high attendance. They can get pretty picky about things like that."

"I'm going to get it. Daddy's going to kill me."

Emily smiled. "Maybe not. Sounds like you've been through a lot." Then, "Mind if I join you up there?"

Lisa's eyes widened. "In the tree?"

"Sure." Emily hadn't meant to frighten or surprise Lisa. Her heart was just so much lighter now that she had found her. And it looked like fun to climb a tree. Emily reached up and grasped the lowest branch. And she was instantly thankful for Amanda's borrowed pair of jeans and sneakers.

"Yeah." As dubious as a teenager could be. "Come on up."

As she swung herself on up into the fork of the trunk, Emily glanced in the direction Philip had disappeared. Maybe she was crazy to climb trees with Philip Manning's thirteen-year-old niece. Then she banished her doubts and followed her instincts. Lisa needed a friend right now, and Emily was willing to participate. She stepped onto a higher branch.

"You climb trees," Lisa stated drily. "I didn't know grown-ups climbed trees."

"Hey. It's been a while. But it's not like we lose the talent. I used to be real good at this."

"Are you a counselor?" Lisa asked quickly. "Dad said if I stepped out of line anymore, he was going to call a counselor and make me talk to her."

"I'm not a counselor. I'm a writer." Emily gazed at the pastoral scene spread below them. "And your home is beautiful. I didn't know a place like this existed, particularly anywhere within a hundred miles of downtown Dallas. It's so quiet here."

Lisa seemed more comfortable with her now that the teenager knew that she did climb trees and she wasn't a counselor. "This used to be…" Lisa struggled to finish her sentence and finally said, "My mother is very sick."

"I know about that," Emily reassured her. "Your uncle told me about it." It was strange calling him that. She still felt as if she should be calling him Mr. Manning.

"This used to be Mom's favorite place on the

whole farm." A restrained reverence filled Lisa's voice. "She used to climb this tree when she was a girl. Sometimes Mom and I would pack a picnic lunch and we'd come down here and hide from everybody and talk."

A pang of regret shot through Emily. *What would it have been like to have a mother to talk to?* "You really miss her, don't you?"

Lisa nodded. "I don't know if she'll ever be coming back."

Emily's heart went out to the girl. She felt the same way about her own mother. But she had given up on their relationship a long, long time ago. Lisa still had hope, and suddenly it seemed to Emily almost more painful that way. "I get the feeling you and your mom were best friends."

"We were." There were tears in Lisa's eyes now. "All my friends at school really liked her, too. She's the only mom who let us stay up all night to see the sunrise when we had a sleepover. Everybody came to the hospital to see her at first. Then they stopped."

"Your mom must be awesome." Emily knew to talk about Amanda in the present tense. She doubted many people did that anymore.

"She wasn't grouchy and she didn't yell like a lot of my friends' moms. She told me that as long as I could find something to laugh about, I could face just about anything that went wrong. Well, I try to find something to laugh about now, and I can't. Ever."

In the distance, a meadowlark sang its throaty scale. A cow lowed over the next hill. Every so often, another pecan hit the ground below them.

"Mom let me have a birthday party here in the pecan grove once." Lisa stared out through the leaves as if she could see into the past. "We started singing songs about boll weevils that Tracy had learned in Texas history. They were so goofy, we started laughing so hard that Amy fell backward into the water trough. So we all went swimming and Tracy's mom got really mad my mom let us get our clothes wet without calling and getting all the other parents' permission and stuff. Tracy's mom wouldn't let her come over here again for a while. But Tracy still says it was the best birthday party she ever went to."

"Are you and Tracy still friends?" Emily asked. The answer to that question was an important one.

Lisa hung her head. "We don't do much together anymore."

"Why not?" Emily swung higher with her arms and, once her feet hit the topmost branch, she stared up at the white cumulus clouds that marched across the sky.

"I don't know," Lisa said carefully. And Emily couldn't help thinking of her own teenage years. She hadn't had many close friends, either. She didn't want the kids in her classes to know about her life at home, so she never invited anyone over. It got so hard pretending to be interested in the petty dramas that the other girls cared about.

"Nobody wants to be around me at school because they don't know what to say. You have to be happy to make people want to talk to you. It's just too hard."

"You know what your mother told you about laughing?" Emily asked. "That's really important. If I were you, I wouldn't be fake about it, but I would do my best to try to find honest things that made me laugh. Laughter can make a person strong." But even as she heard herself giving the girl advice, Emily knew how empty her reassurance sounded. After their prayer beside the house, Emily had no doubt Clint Manning would talk to his daughter differently, about things Emily had long-ago stopped believing. *Trust God. He won't let you down. In the end, you'll be able to look back and see that everything happened for a reason.* Emily wouldn't tell her words like that.

"Your mother would want you to find ways to be happy, to make it happen for yourself."

"Yeah, but it's not that easy." Lisa's gaze shot to Emily's. "If it's so good to make things happen for yourself, why doesn't she just make herself wake up and come home?"

"I don't know," Emily said, "but I'll bet she's trying."

After a thoughtful silence between them, Lisa spoke again. "You remind me a little bit of my mother."

"Why?" Emily was surprised and flattered. "Do I look like her?"

"No." Lisa shook her head. "You don't. But you climb trees. Mom's going to like you when she meets you."

Just as Lisa finished her sentence, there came a very human growl from the base of the tree. "Gr-r-r. I am a big bear that climbs trees."

The voice from below sounded very familiar. Philip. Emily grinned silently at Lisa. He'd returned to the pecan grove and they'd been discovered.

"I love to climb trees," Philip continued in his bear voice. "And I love to eat the things I find in them, particularly when I find little girls who have been skipping school all day long. Gr-r-r."

Lisa couldn't control her giggling anymore, and

Emily laughed outright, too. Suddenly they looked at each other and realized they were both happy despite the conversation they had just finished.

"See," Emily whispered. "It works. All you had to do was wait for some crazy bear to come along."

"Uncle Philip?" Lisa called down to him.

"Gr-r-r," came the reply. And then, with much shrieking and giggling, Lisa swung down to the lower branches and into the fork of the tree, with Emily following. When they both jumped to the ground, Philip looked amazed. And it was Emily who laughed at him.

"I didn't know that girls climbed trees." His voice was halfway teasing, but it held a hint of honest admiration, too.

"Yeah," Emily teased him back. "And I didn't know real estate barons could growl like bears, either."

"Boy, am I glad you're safe." He gripped his niece by the shoulders. Then, to Emily, "You've got me about the bear voice. Just don't tell anyone back in my office."

"I won't," she said with a chuckle. She held up three fingers and made the Girl Scout sign. "Scout's honor."

"Is that where they taught you to climb trees?" Philip Manning looked highly amused that he had found Emily Lattrell in a tree. "In the Girl Scouts?"

"No." She brushed her hands off on the jeans. "That's one of my few amazing talents that I actually taught myself."

Chapter Five

"I don't know what you said to Lisa," Philip told Emily after his niece had skipped on ahead of them toward the house, "but whatever it was, it worked. I haven't seen her happy like this in a long time."

"I don't think it was anything I said to her," Emily admitted. "Your bear imitation is what really made her laugh. And I think she really needed this day of solitude. Girls can be pretty intuitive about themselves. They know what they need to survive." Emily gazed up at him and grinned. She marveled at how easy it was to feel comfortable with him.

The wind blew gently from behind them, and it seemed to push them across the pasture toward the house. Philip's hair fell forward, framing his face. He looked totally at ease and carefree. Three hours before, she could never have imagined the sort of afternoon they would spend together.

"She needed you." Philip couldn't resist touching her with his index finger right on the tip of her nose. It seemed the same gesture he might use with one of Clint's children. He seemed so grateful to Emily for taking the time to come with him to the farm and to help him find Lisa. There had been a hundred other things she might have done this afternoon. And he couldn't have known it, but another woman might have been less compassionate, less able to understand the teenager's grief.

"Maybe she *did* need me." Emily stared off into nothingness as she spoke. "Or maybe she just needed someone to climb trees with her. A monkey could have done that."

"Give yourself more credit than that, Emily. I don't think Amanda ever climbed trees with Lisa."

"You'd be surprised."

Philip stood and watched Emily silently for a moment. Then he grasped her hand. "Come with me." His words were so low that they were almost a whisper. She had shared an important part of herself with him this afternoon. Now he found himself wanting to show her something that was important to him, too.

As they walked toward the twilight together, the

sound of bawling cattle reverberated around them. "Over here." Philip led the way to the base of a lone pecan tree in the meadow where the tall grass grew especially thick. And bedded down there, as if he were sleeping in a nest made just for him, was one tiny white-faced Hereford calf, whose mama was feeding not far away. "This is the farm nursery this fall." He parted the grass to reveal a tiny calf curled up.

"Ah," she gasped. Emily scarcely dared to breathe for fear of frightening it, but when she spoke, the animal just looked at her. Emily took a long moment to examine the pink velvet muzzle and the forehead covered with fluffy furry curls that would never again be quite so white.

"There are two more, a little older, on the other side of the tree. You can see them nosing around." Philip stroked the fuzzy forehead.

Emily's breath caught in her throat as she felt Philip move down closer beside her. For a moment she didn't know why, but she thought he intended to kiss her. He came so close and it would have seemed easy and natural to turn to him. But she didn't. Philip only inspected the calf a bit more closely by running his fingers along one tiny hoof. "This one's a good specimen. Bred from some of the best stock in North Texas."

"Are they all going to make as much noise as their mamas when they grow up?" Emily was desperate to say something, anything, to break the sudden tension that hung in the air between them. The newfound kinship she was feeling with him suddenly frightened her. She had learned a long time ago that it was too painful to become attached to people.

"Yep," Philip said, chuckling. "That and then some. But isn't it a wonderful sound? Cicadas singing and mama cows bawling after their babies."

Philip took her hand and helped her up out of the damp grass. If she'd worried he'd intended to hang on to her hand just a bit longer than was proper, she needn't have. He released her hand quickly, as if he'd gripped something that burned. The mood between the two of them was melancholy as they walked back toward the house. There was a part of Philip that Emily wanted to remember, and she had to wonder whether she'd ever see him again as they tromped wordlessly through the Johnsongrass. After today, Emily had no idea if she'd get another chance to talk to Lisa.

Philip drove her back to Dallas that night, but first he took her and Clint and the kids out for a sandwich at Tom's Bar-B-Q in Waxahachie. Over their meal, Emily had explained to Bethany that she was a writer, that she wrote advertising campaigns for clients and that she dreamed of writing children's books someday.

"What kind of children's books do you want to write?" Bethany asked, and Philip watched Emily answer carefully so his youngest niece with the hearing problem could understand what she was saying. And he wasn't surprised to learn Emily's secret ambition. She seemed childlike and energetic, very much like someone who would write children's books as well as advertising campaigns.

Emily focused on Bethany. "I have some ideas." Then she smiled demurely, but Philip thought he noticed a touch of pride in her expression, too. "My main character is a possum." He guessed she was sharing something that she hadn't shared with many others. "His name is Baby Sprout." She blushed, and it became evident that she didn't want to talk about this part of her fiction-writing career anymore.

Clint was standing to leave, and the rest of them followed suit.

"I think you'd be good writing a story like that," Bethany said.

"I do, too," Lisa chimed in.

"Uncle Philip draws pictures," Bethany said. "He's good, too. You should—" But Philip waved her off and she didn't finish the rest of her sentence.

Emily nodded at the children. “Hm-m-m. I’ll have to find out about those.” She didn’t speak again until Philip held the door for her, and she slid into the car.

“Sorry about that.” She raised her gaze to meet his when he climbed into the front seat beside her.

“For what?”

“For launching into a long dissertation about my dreams.”

If Philip had known her better, he would have teased her about being so unassuming about her talents. *Why is she always so nervous and humble and formal with me?* Her manner set him off balance and intrigued him. Philip was used to meeting people head-on, sparring with them, knowing where he stood with them. But Emily seemed to run forward eagerly toward him and then inexplicably back away. He couldn’t figure out why. “So tell me about your book,” he said, his eyes on the road as they drove along.

“Ha. A successful business mogul like you. Why would you be interested in a children’s book?” She leaned forward and studied his face.

“I have my reasons.” He didn’t know exactly what he should say. He wanted her to tell him something important about herself, too. He could sense that she hadn’t intentionally been mysterious about her aspirations. She just hadn't wanted to talk about them. "Sometimes I think about being an illustrator. Have you really written the stories?"

"I've written one." She sounded almost apologetic. "I haven't submitted it to a publisher."

"Maybe you should."

"Maybe I'm not ready to send it out yet." Privately, Emily knew it didn't need more work. She had been over every word to make certain that it was perfect. But for some reason, she just couldn't let go of it. She couldn't lay another part of herself out there to face rejection.

"What does he look like?"

"Who?"

"Baby Sprout."

"He's a possum," she said. "You must know what possums look like."

"I do." Philip laughed. "We had possums wandering into our garage all the time when Clint and I were boys. We caught one once and named it Fang."

She found it impossible to imagine Philip Manning naming anything Fang. Of course, before this evening it would also have been hard for her to picture him growling up into a tree like a bear, too. But she had just seen him do that.

"Possums are cute and cuddly with teeth that won't quit," Philip said.

"Ignore the teeth part," Emily said. "All those teeth would be too traumatic. We'd be sending kids into therapy. A children's book publisher would never go for that."

Philip shook his head at her. She was dodging his questions again. He wanted her to describe Baby Sprout for him. Bringing her out of herself was becoming a challenge to him. He knew, because of the sincerity he could read in her eyes, that she was not intentionally being vague with him. But when he pulled his car into the driveway of Emily's apartment complex, he still didn't know very much about her. In spite of the spontaneous way she'd responded to Clint's children, he sensed there was something more to her that she didn't let anyone see, a sad undercurrent that he couldn't decipher.

What could she be hiding?

"The barbecue was delicious," she told him as he walked her to her building. "This was a much better adventure than going out for lunch at some fancy restaurant downtown."

As she stood there before him on the walkway, Philip found that same confusing puzzle he'd seen before in her eyes, the openness, the fear. "Emily Lattrell..."

"Yes?"

He rescued himself with the first thing that came to mind. "Promise me you won't tell Lloyd Masterson about my bear imitation."

"No promises." She laughed and the sound of her laughter lingered in the air. "That may be the one story that's too good to pass up." Then, "I had fun today," she told him quietly. Emily felt exhilarated by the day with Philip, by her success at his seminar, by their trip to the farm, by their lively conversation on the way home. Emily had never been brave enough to tell anyone about her Baby Sprout books before. She had done so today because she had seen it as a way to bring Bethany, Clint's younger daughter, into the conversation. Philip's obvious interest in her project didn't seem totally out of character to her now that she had seen how responsive he was to people and how animated he became around his brother's children.

"I'm glad," he said.

Only twelve hours ago, the two of them had only been business acquaintances, and because his niece had disappeared, they had become friends. Friendships did not come easily to Emily. No one really knew that. And she didn't dare try to explain that to him. She wouldn't know where to begin.

"I'm fine," she told him. "You don't have to

walk me up. That's my apartment there." She pointed to a balcony upstairs.

He touched her arm. She recognized it as the same reassuring gesture he had given her in Lloyd's boardroom when she had agreed to do the seminar for him. She searched for her keys in her purse. They jangled in her hand when she turned to him.

"Thank you for today, Philip Manning." Her voice was low.

He grabbed her arm to keep her from turning away from him. "I'm the one who should be thanking you, Emily." He was so close to her that he was looking straight down at her. "But thanking you doesn't seem to be enough."

She threw her head back again and laughed. She couldn't help thinking that it was ironic, Philip being so grateful. It had been such an honor for her to spend the day with him. It seemed like an eternity ago when she had wended her way through the crowd toward him at the seminar. He had seemed so much larger than life to her that morning, because of the things she knew about his career and his prominent status in business. Now he seemed more and less of the man she'd thought him to be. She had seen him as a human being against the backdrop of a place that he loved. And in a way, knowing him made her feel more confident about herself, about the fact that she was a human being with feelings and insecurities, too. It surprised her how at ease she felt with him, remembering how his reputation had intimidated her.

She smiled up at him and he felt the strangest feeling then, as if Emily had been sent to him by some discerning force to prove to him that his life was devoid of something very important, indeed. He was still unconsciously gripping her arm, as if by holding on to her he might be able to hold on to a possibility he had lost a long time before.

He bent toward her and cradled the back of her head against his palm. He wanted her to know how thankful he was for the things she had done. But there was more to it, too. Suddenly he didn't want to leave her.

Emily's eyes widened as she searched his face. His hesitation answered countless questions that she hadn't dared to ask. The day had been a special one for him, too. And perhaps the attraction she'd felt for him was mutual. She didn't say anything to him, but she didn't step away. She only stood before him, with her keys dangling from her hand.

"What is it?" she asked. "Why are you looking at me like that?"

"I was just thinking about you in that tree this afternoon," he said. And the indecision he was feeling registered in his voice. "I was thinking how very different you are from other women I've known."

"Because I climb trees?" She gave him an impish grin.

"Because of everything you did today," he told her earnestly. "That, and plenty of other reasons." After Morgan had betrayed him, Philip had risked his heart one more time. He'd met a woman, Erin, in a singles' Bible study at church, who he'd finally been able to talk to.

He'd finally been able to talk to Erin about his family and the conflicts he'd felt running a competitive business and being a Christian man. After they'd gone out for coffee and for dinner a couple of times, Philip had prayed for the Father to show him whether or not Erin might be the woman God intended him to spend his life with. He'd followed his emotions with Morgan, this time he would plan it out with his head.

The next day, Erin told him she'd be leaving for training to be a missionary in Poland. When she'd seen him nod with his knowing look, she'd smiled and asked, "What's that expression for?"

"Oh," he'd told her, "just an answer to prayer, is all."

She'd lifted her chin and said, "You know, Philip. God doesn't always call us to spend our lives with someone else. Sometimes he calls us to stay alone so we can be closer to Him."

To this day, Philip wasn't sure whether Erin had meant those words for herself or whether she'd meant them for *him.* He had taken them that way; he had taken them for his own.

He had no idea where Emily stood in her faith. Philip didn't expect to need anyone to share his life. But if he *did* end up with someone, he knew the Heavenly Father wanted him to find a woman who trusted Him with all her being. He'd seen Emily be so kind with his nieces and nephew, and that counted for so much. But he had no idea how she felt about God.

"It's easy to see how much you love those kids," Emily said, bringing him back.

"They're everything I have," he told her.

"Don't forget your real estate company," she said, teasing.

And he said, "Emily," his voice so low that she barely heard him. "My life isn't as uncomplicated or as magical as that."

"No? I don't believe you," she said solemnly. "You make success look so easy."

"It isn't easy." His eyes locked on hers, and the ice-blue color of them seemed to beckon to her, to pull her longings out of her heart. Her other memories of the day dissipated. She only remembered him and the way he looked at her and the wonderful tingle that had surged through her when she thought he was going to kiss her.

"I should go," he said quietly. "I've monopolized your entire day."

"It was wonderful," she said, and he noticed that there was a certain sadness in her voice, as if she was already looking back on their time together as a distant memory. And Philip didn't quite know what he should say. He hardly knew her.

Emily put her key in the lock, then she went outside and stood on the balcony and waved at him as he drove off. And then she stood for a long time, feeling alone and unsatisfied in the darkness, staring down the street to the horizon where his car had disappeared, to where the streetlights cast a rose-colored hue on the asphalt below.

"Abbie Carson is in the front office to see you, Emily," her secretary informed her over the intercom.

"Who?"

"Abbie Carson."

Emily tried to remember why that name sounded familiar.

"Abbie Carson with Absolutely Moms."

"Oh." Thank goodness she'd gotten a prompt.

"*Oh.* Of course." The woman Philip had told her about. "Send her in."

A gray-haired, jovial woman appeared in the doorway and moved to grip Emily's hand firmly in her own. "Just happened to be driving by and I took the chance I might be able to talk face-to-face with you. I left my cell phone lying on my desk in the office. We're still a little unorganized over there." Abbie Carson radiated energy.

"I saw one of your brochures a few days ago," Emily said, motioning to the chair across her desk. "I'd love to chat with you."

"Actually, that's why I came by." Abbie sat and didn't mince words. "I need to redo the brochure, now that we're in Dallas, too." The woman didn't waste time with polite or trivial conversation. Every move, every word, was economical. It was obvious how this one woman had accomplished so much in one short lifetime. "Philip Manning said you were the person for the job. We have tremendous potential to help people in Texas."

Emily pulled a notepad from the top drawer of her desk. "I heard about your plans here. I'd like to hear about it in your own words, though." It had been three days since Emily had spent the day with Philip Manning. For three days Emily had done her best to get him out of her mind. At first, just thinking of the conversations she'd had with Philip made it hard for Emily to concentrate on the things Abbie was saying. But as the woman continued telling her story, Emily couldn't help but become involved in it.

"My business started fourteen years ago when my husband died," Abbie told her. "I was in my forties with three grown children and no real goals for the future. An acquaintance whose wife had died begged me to move in with him and become an adopted mother to his two sons, aged eight and twelve."

"What a challenge." Emily sipped from the coffee mug on her desk.

"Believe it or not, it worked. My two new 'sons' and I had wonderful adventures every afternoon. We fished in the Potomac River, visited the Smithsonian Institute and spent days at the zoo. We did everything there was to do in Washington, D.C., where my first 'surrogate family' lived."

"I can see how something like that would give you a new lease on life."

"You bet it did. After we ran out of things to do in Washington, D.C., we went to New York and spent a day there riding everything that moved—the ferry, the subway, a taxi." Abbie's eyes sparkled as she spoke; her joy seemed to come from loving children and doing childlike things. Emily could picture this woman dragging two little boys throughout a city, hailing cabs, catching trains, boarding boats. Emily had to grin. She was surprised Abbie and the boys hadn't figured out how to fly in an airplane and how to ride in a helicopter, too.

"After I'd spent one summer with those kids, their neighbors were all asking what I had done," Abbie confided, and Emily found herself wanting to soak up the enthusiasm. Here was a woman who was doing something noteworthy with her life. Abbie's being a replacement mom touched a chord somewhere deep in Emily. Her *own* mother had been absent, even though she'd often been in the same room. Oh, how Emily would have loved to have known someone like Abbie Carson then. "Everyone said my boys were so much happier with themselves, that they seemed so much more secure. That's when I began to realize that if two children could change so drastically with simple discipline and love, there must be many more families out there somewhere who needed a full-time, managerial, professional mother."

No wonder Philip Manning had been so impressed with Abbie Carson. The woman was so intent on her own cause, so certain of the work she was doing. A diminutive, vivacious woman, Abbie Carson might be destined to lead a great many other women and children to happiness. Motherhood. She had taken something that, by today's standards, could be termed "old-fashioned" and had turned it into something very, very new.

Abbie had served as an "adopted mom" for five different families, during the next eight years, she said. God used her to create a blessing and the kids blessed her back. "A natural mother has no salary, no time off and she also does the scrubbing, the vacuuming and the ironing. An Absolutely Mom cheers at Little League baseball games, goes to school plays and piano recitals. She even teaches kids how to bake cookies."

"It sounds like the hired mom gets all the fun parts." *If God could be trusted, why would He have given me a mother who didn't want to do fun things like that with me?* Emily couldn't push the nagging question away.

"Oh, she does the other parts, too." Abbie ticked them off on her fingers as she named them. "She does the meal planning, the budgeting, buys clothes for the children, keeps things in order and is hired to be a problem solver, a manager, an organizer. She has the weekends off if she wants them, and she receives a paycheck. She is not a housekeeper."

"She isn't?"

"We have fathers who want our services so badly that they'll spend the money on us rather than a cleaning lady. Even if they have to come home and do the scrubbing themselves on the weekends."

"That says a whole lot."

"It *does.* I started off like a fire horse that heard the bell. I knew the time had come to spark other people's interest. And it was easy. I had done it myself."

"It's a wonderful idea."

"When the time came, it was easy for me to talk to other women about it. I was the one who had all the fun. I was the one who had sat around in the firelight reading the children stories and loving them."

God? If other mothers want to do this, then why didn't mine?

Absolutely Moms was a nonprofit corporation with offices in Arlington, Virginia, and Carmel and Palo Alto, California. Abbie worked now as the company administrator, constantly matching her mothers with families who needed them. To date, she had placed over two thousand mothers all around the world.

"Well?" When Abbie finished speaking, she noticed a faraway, intense expression in Emily's eyes. She had seen that wistful expression in women's eyes plenty of times before. These professional women thought they had it all. But they didn't. Not by half. She asked tentatively, "What about the brochure? Will you do it for me?"

"Of course," Emily answered softly. But even Abbie's question couldn't break her reverie. In her mind, she was far, far away…in a grassy pasture with baby calves and bawling mamas. She was thinking of Clint's children and wondering what a difference an Absolutely Mom would make for Clint and the Manning clan. And she was wondering what a difference an Absolutely Mom could have made in her own life, for her father, for them all.

"Do you have a hard time finding women to do this, Abbie?"

"There are many reasons to become an Absolutely Mom." Abbie's voice turned suddenly gentle. She had grown accustomed to redirecting lives and channeling women in the directions they needed to go. "Maybe a woman feels like something is missing in her life and maybe she wants to find something more. Or maybe she wants to give to someone else what she herself could never have…

"I have four women placed right now who hold doctorates in various disciplines. Some people say they're overqualified for this. But I say, if you love being a mother, you can't be overqualified. You pass all that you are on to the children. You share your creativity. You share your wealth of experience."

"So, I guess you have all the mothers you need."

"Oh, no." Abbie's laughter was like a gentle bell that tinkled throughout the room. "I told you we have lots of mothers. But we never have enough. I have a mile-long waiting list of families who need mothers."

Emily sighed. Three days ago she had been with children who desperately needed the services and the love that only a mother could offer. And she knew how important that could be because she had lived a life that had been sadly devoid of that love, too.

Abbie was standing to leave, and Emily stood as well to take her hand. "I'd be honored to update your brochure for you."

"Good." Abbie handed her a business card with her new Dallas address already printed on it. "That's my landline number and my cell phone right there."

"I'll call you when I have something for you to look at." Emily hoped she and Abbie Carson could become friends. She felt strangely drawn to her. "Or maybe when I get the copy done, I'll just come over to your place. I'd love to see the Absolutely Moms offices."

Abbie grinned. "I'd like that, too."

After the woman left, Emily sat for a long time thinking, wondering what type of person gave up everything they had, their careers and their homes, to become an Absolutely Mom. A woman who had nothing left to prove professionally; that was for sure. A woman who trusted something beyond herself, to guide her into touching someone else's life. A woman who *trusted...*

Emily rose from her chair, walked to her filing cabinet in the corner. *That wouldn't be me.* She thumbed through her files. She had trouble finding the one she wanted, but finally the right one fell open before her, and Emily pulled it out of the drawer. The Baby Sprout file.

She laid it on her desk. The folder contained one of her greatest dreams. She had been working on this project off and on during her lunch hours for months. And one day when she could screw up the courage, she was going to submit it to a children's book publisher. Just talking to Abbie Carson and seeing how the woman had found the courage to start her life over had made Emily want to start working on her book again.

In Emily's manuscript, Baby Sprout the possum befriended a nine-year-old girl named Priscilla. Priscilla thought she should be allowed to grow up and become a princess. Together the two of them set out to prove to old Judge Wyland that Priscilla ought to be a princess and have a throne to perch on in the middle of the town square. The two of them are waylaid time after time because Priscilla's mother keeps asking her to fold the socks from the dryer.

It had all started as a funny, ironic tale in Emily's mind and it had remained there and taken shape until it had become something much more important. It had become the story of a young child who needed to find acceptance and love from the people who surrounded her. It had come to be her own mythical autobiography.

Is that why I work so hard at the ad agency? Do I try to prove to others how much I'm worth?

Then, there was Philip. Emily found herself attracted to Philip for a great many reasons. He was handsome and kind and she had seen his compassion.

She had to wonder: *Am I drawn to this man because he gives me worth? Because I like how he looks at me professionally?* All the wrong reasons for starting a relationship with someone.

Even that word, *relationship,* terrified her, conjured up painful images in her mind, memories of nights her father had waited up for her mother, the nights his diligence had been paid off by a swaggering wife who hurled insults and profanities at him with the same force that she would have hurled rocks. Emily's greatest fear was that she might spend her life in a relationship as hopeless as the one her parents had shared: her father, never knowing if his wife would be sober, or ready to send him reeling with her accusations, or if she'd even bother to come home; her mother, always angry, always unhappy, driven by an addiction she couldn't control.

Emily knew that alcoholism, and addictive traits in general, were something she might inherit. If she let herself give in, she felt terrified that she might develop those tendencies. Emily decided she'd rather live her life alone than experience such disillusionment and pain.

Philip Manning rocked back in his studio chair and made several short, light strokes with his charcoal pencil. He filled in with shading, used the pungent eraser to smudge the strokes, darkened a spot with the pencil here and there, then held it up so he could examine his work. *Hm-m-mm.* Not bad.

Philip was drawing again. He could relax here in his studio on the second floor of his Walnut Hill condominium. He knew the drawings he produced in this room would never win any major art awards, but he loved them because they were his therapy. No one who knew him in the outside world would guess that he kept great stacks of pictures piled around the room. Some were serious sketches of pastoral scenes he loved at the farm—windmills, cattle, the old house. Others were silly and full of fantasy, sketches of swirling clouds in the night sky or caricatures of people.

No matter what the subject matter of his drawings, they all served the same purpose for him. Working with newsprint and a handful of soft pencils made him briefly forget the multimillion-dollar properties and the clients that demanded services from him each day.

This evening, Philip had started out drawing a pecan tree and a calf. That had been a mistake. Every time he pictured the tree, he thought of Emily Lattrell. Every time he pictured the calf, he thought of how Emily had looked, crouched in the Johnsongrass beside the newborn calf in the pasture. It was a game he had been unwittingly allowing himself to play for three days now, thinking of Emily by association. He played it when he talked to Lisa on the telephone, when he glanced for the umpteenth time at the copy Emily had written for his brochure.

Thinking of Emily so often was making him crazy. He decided to change his strategy. Might as well wallow in his thoughts, to do his best to think of her so much that he would get enough of her. He started out by taking his sketch pad and working on a drawing of the possum she had described, the possum in her book named Baby Sprout.

Then, after he had started working on the character, his idea had taken form. At the office that morning, Philip had prepared a list of associates and friends for his secretary to send thank-you notes to for their participation in his seminar. When he had jotted Emily Lattrell's name on that list, his hand had paused. He wanted to give Emily more than just a formal note of thanks.

He thought of all the tokens of appreciation he could send her. Flowers? A gift certificate to a restaurant? Stationery? Nothing seemed quite right until he found himself in his studio, pacing the floor, inexplicably thinking about Emily's dreams of writing a children's book.

Suddenly he couldn't get the image of her face out of his mind. She had been so demure and dainty talking to him that day at the farm about her dreams, so unlike the cool professional she'd been earlier. It was hard for him to imagine a woman as feminine as Emily creating a possum as an imaginary character for a book. Philip had grown up thinking that girls didn't know a thing about possums and crawdads and fishing.

He did his best to remember everything Emily had told him about the book's character, and as he stopped sketching, Philip finally felt satisfied. He liked the way drawing something for her made him feel close to her again.

He made several changes as he worked. He eventually gave up on the elongated nose and made Baby Sprout's nose a tad squarer. He made the eyes less beady, drawing them larger and rounder instead. He made the white part of Baby Sprout's face fuzzy and soft.

Philip did his best to suggest the things he knew of Emily's personality—her spontaneity, her willingness to give—in the character. And by the time Philip had completed his sketch of "a possum of all things," he had become totally absorbed in the work he had done.

He propped Baby Sprout on his easel, strolled across the room and examined it from afar.

Not for a minute did he stop to wonder if this might be a presumptuous gift to send her. Philip was accustomed to doing what others might call presumptuous things. That's the way he'd made it big in Dallas, following his instincts.

That's all this is, Philip reminded himself. *I'm doing this to thank a colleague, no other reason.*

Erin's words rang out in his head. *God doesn't always call us to spend our lives with someone else.*

Morgan's betrayal still weighed heavy as a millstone on his heart.

He tucked the charcoal drawing inside his briefcase and carried it to a shop near the office to have it framed. After he'd picked it up again, he propped it on the shelf in his office, wondering when the right time would come to take it to her.

Emily had notes spread across her kitchen table Saturday morning when her doorbell rang. She hurried to the door with several papers in her hand and a pencil stuck behind her left ear. Philip chuckled at her when she swung the door open and stared at him.

"Hello," he said.

Emily's hand stayed the door. She had tried so hard to forget him. And now here he was. "Philip. What are you doing here?"

"Should I have called?" he asked. "Is this a bad time? Are you working, Emily?"

"I'm working on Abbie Carson's brochure." Her hand held the door against him for one beat. Two.

"Do you mind if I come in?"

"No," she lied. But inside she was thinking, *I don't want to care about you.*

When Philip followed her into her apartment, he placed the package he'd been carrying on the floor beside the sofa.

"How's your family?" she asked, and she hated herself for sounding tentative, as if she didn't know if she had the right to ask about them or not.

"Much better. Clint's decided to give Lisa the okay to take that field trip in a few weeks. Lisa convinced him to talk to one of the mothers who's chaperoning. Clint has a hard time letting go. He's worried something's going to take them away from him the same way something took Amanda."

Emily hesitated, then said, "All of us do that, don't you think? All of us let something that hurt us before affect the way we see people now."

He froze. "What are you talking about, Emily?" *Morgan. Erin.* She might as well have told him she could see into his very soul.

"Nothing. It just—" She shook her head. "I'm not talking about anything important. I'm glad Lisa's going on the trip."

"I think it's okay, too," Philip said. "Lisa's a responsible girl."

Emily walked to the kitchen table and picked up

the copy she had been working on. "Abbie Carson came to my office this week. Thank you for sending her." Emily hesitated again. She had so many personal questions to ask him, questions that, for some reason, she felt uncomfortable asking him now. She didn't want to pry. "Has Clint called her yet?"

"No. I decided not to push him."

"I wish he would."

"I do, too," Philip agreed. Then, unceremoniously, he shoved the brown paper package into her hands. "I brought this for you."

Emily took it from him, all the while watching him, trying to figure out why he had come. "You didn't need to do anything."

He grinned at her. "Yes, I did."

She didn't open it. She just pondered the boyish expression on his face.

"Go ahead. It's a present. Open it."

She ripped open the brown paper and pulled back the tissue. At first she didn't realize what the sketch was supposed to be. She thought it was a picture he had bought for her. And when she saw the charcoal drawing, she decided he had stumbled on a picture of a possum somewhere, and thinking of Baby Sprout, he had bought it for her.

She propped the drawing on the shelf and stepped away from it. "Thank you for the picture, Philip." She glanced at him from over her shoulder. He probably thought her odd because she had created a character that was a possum.

She examined the picture further, and realized how much of it pleased her. She didn't want to seem silly, but Emily had the strangest feeling that she was peering into the face of an old friend. The possum in the drawing looked exactly as she'd imagined Baby Sprout.

"You're going to think I'm crazy," she said, "but this is a picture of Baby Sprout. Where did you find it?"

When he didn't answer, Emily turned toward him. "Where did you find this?" she asked again, unable to contain her excitement.

"You think it looks like Baby Sprout?" he asked. "Is the nose right? It's more square than a real possum's nose. But it gives so much personality to his face, I thought."

Emily studied the creature's nose before she answered him. "Yes. Absolutely. It's perfect." She turned her eyes up toward his. "You know," she told him, "you'll probably think I'm crazy, but, Philip, it's uncanny how much like my Baby Sprout this possum really looks."

"Oh." Philip's voice stayed steady and noncommittal. He didn't want to give himself away, not until she realized he was the artist.

"The strange thing is—" Emily hesitated, pacing the floor. "I wasn't certain myself how Baby Sprout was supposed to look. I had an idea in my head of how other people were supposed to perceive him. But if someone had asked me to describe this, I wouldn't have been able to do it."

"Is there anything about this drawing that you would change?" Philip asked.

"I doubt it." She considered the sketch again. "But maybe his legs. I might make his hind legs shorter and fuller. Through here." She ran one finger down the possum's hind leg. When she did, she spied the signature. P. B. Manning.

"Here's the artist's signature," Emily said. It seemed a miracle that someone she didn't know had created a picture that fit her vision so perfectly. Emily would have to find the artist and…

She stopped. The initials on the sketch. "P. B. Manning."

Bethany's words came to mind from the evening she had met his family. *Uncle Philip draws pictures. He's good, too.*

She froze with the picture in her hand and stared at him. *Philip Manning!*

"What's your middle name, Philip?" Her voice was quavering.

"Bradley," he told her.

In a flash, Emily realized what a gift Philip had brought her. The sketch *was* Baby Sprout. And he had drawn it for her. Tears came to her eyes. She felt for a moment as if Philip had taken her dream and had drawn it and made it real.

"You did this." A statement, not a question. There was no doubt in Emily's mind. She had seen his signature. And now she knew why the drawing was so appropriate, so nearly what she wanted. This wasn't a coincidence.

"I never can decide whether I should put the B for Bradley on there, or not."

Turning from him, Emily plopped on the sofa with the drawing in her hands. And Philip was surprised when he saw the tears of emotion in her eyes.

"Emily, don't. You don't need to cry." He sat beside her on the sofa. "It isn't that bad, is it?"

She turned her face up to his, and he felt terrible that she was distressed. Maybe she thought he had tricked her. But she was smiling at him through her tears. "Hey, I cry when I'm happy, too, Philip." She reached over and gingerly touched his knee. "I can't believe you did this. This is one of the nicest things anyone has ever done for me. I don't know what to say. I don't. Thank you."

Privately, he wondered if maybe he had done something that was too personal. Maybe he had overstepped his bounds. But he realized he had given a face to something that was very, very important to her.

"How did you know how to draw him?"

"You told me." His eyes were wide, and his expression made it seem as if her telling him had been simple.

"I couldn't have." Emily shook her head. "I didn't know myself."

"No. When an artist works, he relies on things he feels inside to give his characters their depth and personality. When I designed Baby Sprout, I thought about who you are, Emily."

"Tell me about his eyes." Emily sat on her hands and perched higher up beside him on the sofa. "How did you figure out how to draw his eyes?"

Philip looked at her, his expression playful. It was her eyes he saw then, gazing up at him expectantly from her round little-girl face. She looked so beautiful to him, so happy and expectant, that he wondered if, in trying to bring her such a special gift, he had brought her something she thought she didn't deserve and had never expected.

"Sometimes you have to do things a certain way just because they seem right. Do you mind, Emily?" It had been a long time since he'd followed his intuition like this. "Maybe I shouldn't have drawn this. I didn't mean to detract from anything you've planned or created."

"No." She pulled one hand from beneath her and touched his arm to reassure him. Baby Sprout had sprung to life for her today. "No." The second time she negated his doubts it was for a stronger reason, not just because she wanted to reassure Philip, but because she felt that, in some way, Baby Sprout was better, that she knew him now, because Philip had worked on him, too.

"Do you know anything about illustrating children's books?" she asked him. "Do you know if publishers want to see artwork when a writer submits a story?"

"I'm not sure." He shrugged. He'd never considered making his work public. "I suppose if you had an idea in mind…"

"When we submit a television commercial to a client, we have one of the artists at the agency do storyboards. Would you submit storyboards with a manuscript?"

"Don't know." He shrugged again. He still didn't know what she was getting at.

"Philip." She turned toward him now, and she was demure and yet businesslike when she made her suggestion. "Would you be willing to do some storyboards for Baby Sprout? If my book ever gets published, I want Baby Sprout to look exactly like this." She held Philip's work at arm's length and smiled.

"You would want me to do that?" He was pleased, but the idea would take some getting used to. "Wouldn't you rather have a professional artist? It could make a difference between having your book published or not."

"Philip," she began, then paused to emphasize the importance of her words. "We've created something together. Right now, it feels like I came up with Baby Sprout and then you became involved and made him even better. I'm willing to share the limelight." She realized as she coaxed him that if she convinced him to do the artwork she would be obligated to submit her work to a publisher. But that was okay, she reasoned, because she was finally willing to commit to her dream, thanks to Philip.

"Emily." Philip couldn't say more. He was overcome by the fact that she liked his work so much, and that she trusted him enough to place a dream in his hands.

He sensed something about her, something unseen, that made him want to win victories for her.

He turned to Emily then, and he grabbed her hand and pulled her up off of the sofa before he gave her his answer. And Emily was suddenly so excited that she didn't flinch or pull away. "Okay, let's collaborate," he said.

He looked down at her and felt as if an entirely new world was opening up for him. He couldn't resist telling her, "You think it's going to be more fun working on Baby Sprout than finalizing multimillion-dollar real estate sales?"

"It might be more fun. But you won't get rich from it. That's for certain."

"You never know," he commented wryly. "I want my share of the royalties, too."

"Oh?" She raised her eyebrows. "This could be a wonderful working relationship. Don't go getting greedy on me."

"I'll do my best." He winked at her, then turned suddenly somber. "I'm serious, though. Doing things like this, being creative, thinking about people, means so much more to me than just sitting in my office concocting deals."

"So why didn't you start out as a book illustrator or a social worker?" she asked. "Sounds to me like you jumped headfirst into an all-consuming business."

"I did," he told her. "It was what was expected

of me, I suppose." *No, it was what Morgan expected of me.* "Why are you asking anyhow? I did the same thing you've done."

"I know," she said, nodding. "I guess that's why I asked you the question." Emily couldn't help thinking of Abbie Carson, of the people-oriented business the woman had established, the business that counted its assets in love and discipline and children's futures rather than in dollars and cents.

"What is it?" Philip asked. He couldn't guess what she must be thinking, but he knew her mind must be someplace far away. He took her face in his hands, and for some reason, he looked different to Emily then, as if he had grown younger, as if he had grown carefree. He searched her face with his eyes as he smiled at her, and she wanted to cry out from the sheer sensation of his nearness. He was looking at her like a little boy who had just brought home his first bicycle.

"Philip," she said softly, and the tears came to her eyes again, this time because she knew she had to push him away.

He had his hands beneath her hair, on the back of her neck. And all Emily wanted to do was close her eyes and let him kiss her. But Emily couldn't let that happen. She couldn't let him reach out to her this way. He had brought her the sketch of

Baby Sprout and he had brought his friendship, and she couldn't jeopardize the things they were sharing in the hope that they might find more. Feeling this way, hoping this way, didn't last. Emily's parents had proved that to her. "No, Philip." Emily wedged her palms up between them. "Don't do this."

And even if things like this *did* last, Emily knew—because of what she'd learned in childhood—she wasn't worthy of having a man like this pursue and romance her.

As Philip looked down at her, it was the first time that he consciously realized he was touching her. And it surprised him, as he studied her face, that he wasn't thinking of Morgan at all. He could only think of Emily in his arms. She seemed so open to him, so alive. And as she pushed her arms up against his shoulders, he only wanted to protect her, to shield her from her loneliness.

"Don't push me away, Emily," he said, and the blue in his eyes turned to ice when it mixed with the resolve that welled up in them.

"I have to, Philip." She turned her face away from him and pressed it into his shoulder. It was too late, though. Philip had already seen the fear in her eyes.

"Why?" He gripped her by the shoulders and

pushed her back so he could read her expression. "What are you afraid of?"

"I'm not afraid of anything. It's nothing."

He cupped her head in his hands and turned her toward him a second time. "Don't tell me that." His voice rumbled low in his throat. "Don't tell me it's nothing."

She saw the anger in his eyes and it frightened her, but it gave her more strength to stand up for what she believed was right. Anger was a familiar emotion to her. It was an emotion that, in her experience, went hand in hand with love. "What do you want from me, Philip?" Her voice went thick with conviction. "Why are you really here?" She reached up and took his hands from her face. She held them in her own while she spoke. "I think you should go."

"I'm threatening something in you, is that it? Do you want to tell me what it is, Emily?"

She pulled away from him, and the drawing of Baby Sprout, propped on the shelf, seemed to be jeering at her. When she spun toward Philip, he saw the desperation in her eyes.

Philip had thought Emily might be someone he could depend on. But she reminded him of Morgan Brockner when she talked of the things she didn't want. And he felt betrayed because when he'd been with her before, she'd been so different.

Betrayal. With that one word came the memories of Morgan's treachery. The morning he'd walked into the empty office. The calculated way she'd built their business partnership under the guise of romance. The announcement of Morgan's new venture in the *Dallas Morning News.*

Why won't I ever learn, Lord? When I let my defenses down, something always comes to remind me. This road has been hard, maybe because You don't call me to walk it.

And here he'd been, discussing a book-illustration project with Emily Lattrell!

"There's no need to be afraid of this," he said as much to himself as to her, his voice hard. "I am a Christian man and I don't plan to dishonor you or lead you astray."

"Oh." She shifted her weight from one hip to another. *"Oh."* Then, after a horrible period of silence, she finished it. "If you're one of those churchgoing types, then I *really* don't want anything to do with it."

So there is my answer, Lord, he thought.

"I don't want to lead you on." She flipped her hair behind her shoulder. "I have no intention of trying to drag you into a courtship with me."

"Who said anything about a courtship?" Philip's pride spoke now. Talking to Emily like this, when she was so stubbornly unyielding, provoked feelings like those he had experienced trying to reason with Morgan. Only it had been different with Morgan. This conversation with Emily felt infinitely more frustrating. At least with Morgan he might have had a chance. But Emily wouldn't give an inch. Philip turned away from her and stared at the funny, friendly little possum he had drawn for her. He didn't see the hurt in her eyes.

She said, "Why don't you take the artwork back? I would feel awkward keeping it."

"No. It's yours. I wouldn't have any reason to want it." Philip went to the door and took hold of the knob before he turned to face her. "I'm sorry, Emily," he told her. "I shouldn't have come."

She didn't answer him. She just stared at him as he stood with his fist clenched around the doorknob.

Then, "No. You shouldn't have."

As she watched him go, she knew he deserved so much more than she would ever be able to give him. That thought, when it came to her, was the one that gave Emily final resolve. She walked to the doorway and closed the door behind him. Then she picked up the portrait of Baby Sprout and stared at it in silence until she heard Philip's car roaring away below.

Chapter Six

Emily arrived at Abbie Carson's office early. She did her best not to think about Philip and the things she had said to him while she waited in the front room of the Absolutely Moms office. One entire wall in the front room was covered with photographs—large ones, small ones, professional portraits and quick family snapshots, all of children. Children smiling and playing and posing. The joy in their faces made them all look similar, as if they were all cousins or sisters and brothers sharing in the same family. And in a way they were, Emily knew.

Her mind wandered back to something Abbie had told her during their first meeting, something about being with children, something about becoming an Absolutely Mom. *Maybe you feel like some-*

thing is missing in your own life. Or maybe you just want to give to someone else what you never could have....

The idea of becoming an Absolutely Mom was opposed to the things Emily thought she wanted—the golden plaques on the wall, the marketing seminars, the statistics. But she was beginning to understand the emptiness of pursuing money and professional recognition. The sketch Philip had drawn for her kept taunting her, reminding her of the dreams she had forgotten to follow. She didn't want the superficiality of living for plaques and awards anymore.

If she could only embark on living for someone else, something where she could share herself for others, to be more than her mother had been for her, maybe she could put the past behind her. Maybe she could start to heal.

She wanted to stop striving, to stop trying to prove to herself that she was worth something.

When Abbie entered the room to greet her, Emily handed her the brochure. "What do you think?" she asked after she'd given Abbie time to read over her work.

Abbie nodded, obviously pleased. "Now I know why Philip Manning recommended you. You've done a good job, captured everything I wanted to say in these few graphs." Abbie hesitated. She waited, as if she thought Emily might want something else.

Emily went over the billing procedure for her brochure work. She double-checked the printing schedule to make certain both she and Abbie were on the same page. Then Emily hesitated, too, knowing she could not postpone what she'd come for any longer. She knew what she wanted to do. She wanted to stop hiding behind her career. "May I fill out an application to be an Absolutely Mom, Abbie?" Emily wondered if she sounded abrupt, as she often did when she felt nervous. What if Abbie Carson didn't think she was qualified? She would feel like an utter fool.

But Abbie didn't respond the way Emily had expected. She did not ask, "Are you certain you want to do this?" the way anyone else would have.

"Would you be willing to move in with a family?" Abbie asked. "I'd need you to do that."

Emily didn't hesitate. She wanted it desperately. She suddenly realized she wanted this more than anything. "Yes."

"I have paperwork for you to fill out, then. I'll need your references. Although, knowing you the way I do, I don't anticipate there will be any problems."

"I imagine there's a waiting period."

"It's important to our families that we check backgrounds thoroughly."

Emily nodded in acceptance.

"And, after I have your résumé and references in hand, we'll have another in-depth interview. It's important you know what is expected."

Emily gripped the packet in both hands.

Two weeks after Emily had pored over the application and gone through two interviews with Abbie and her references had all recommended her heartily, Abbie phoned Emily to congratulate her and tell her she had a position.

Emily drove to the agency to give Lloyd her two weeks' notice. And when she did, Lloyd was furious. He didn't understand why she was leaving. At first, he was certain she was becoming an Absolutely Mom out of spite, because he hadn't agreed to put the snorkeler and the bride in the city train ads.

By three o'clock Lloyd had calmed down enough to talk to her. But when he asked her again why she had to leave, Emily didn't know how to tell him what it was that she longed for. She only knew that she wanted to share a portion of her life with someone who needed her, that she wanted to embark on a journey.

"Don't come running back to me when you realize the error you've made." Lloyd slid his glasses down his nose and eyed her without the aid of his lenses. "There won't ever be another job here for you, Emily, if you decide to leave this way."

"I have to take my chances, then." She locked her measured gaze on his. "I have to resolve this for myself, Lloyd," she told him. "I don't need a professional career right now. I need something more."

Emily kept herself sane the next two weeks by sorting belongings and packing them away for storage. Shoes went into the "take" box. Pans and magazines went into the "Dad's basement" box. Eggs, vegetables and half a gallon of milk went into a container Emily planned to leave for the neighbor.

She finished packing at noon on Friday. Exhausted from the effort of getting everything into crates and the emotional strain of changing her life on what now seemed like a whim, she went to bed. She slept late the next morning, rushed to have breakfast and dress, and by lunchtime, Abbie Carson knocked on her door. When Emily opened it, Abbie handed Emily three long-stemmed roses wrapped in paper. "You have a family, Emily," Abbie told her quietly, her eyes shining with emotion. "You now are the adopted mother of three children. One rose for each child."

Before Emily could even take the roses, Abbie launched into a description of her new life. She would be living in a cabin with its own small kitchen. It seemed like the perfect place to have a white wicker rocking chair and a sweep-off porch for sunning on the south side of the house.

"Where is this place?" Emily asked, suddenly feeling like an expectant child. She hadn't felt this way since she'd been a little girl, playing house. And perhaps, she mused, she was doing exactly the same thing. Abbie had certainly made it sound like the experience would be similar. "Is it near here?" Emily asked. Then, without waiting for an answer, she breathed, "Tell me about the children."

"It's a good drive from here, down south in Ellis County near Waxahachie. You'll be living on a farm. The father's name is Clint Manning."

Abbie kept talking, but after that Emily didn't hear a word she said. Emily's blood turned to ice. All she could comprehend was the relentless pounding in her ears. The Mannings. Abbie had put her with the Mannings, to take Amanda's place with Philip's nieces and nephew.

I can't do it, Emily thought. *This is a mistake.*

Clint Manning had no idea who he had just hired to take over as a mother in his household. Emily could only guess that Clint had finally called Abbie and that either Abbie had no idea the Waxahachie Mannings were related to the Philip Manning she knew in Dallas or else Abbie didn't think it important that they were. She couldn't have known about the day Emily had already spent with them on the farm.

Then, almost immediately, her panic disappeared. The more Emily thought of it, the more feasible the position on the Manning farm began to sound. There was nothing between her and Philip, anyway. They'd only been business acquaintances for a very short time. And Emily decided she would love to accept the position on the farm in Waxahachie. She guessed she might be living in the cabin she'd seen in the pecan grove, and she could picture everything just the way it had been the day she had found Lisa in the tree.

Lisa. Lisa could be perhaps her biggest challenge and her greatest joy.

As if on cue, Abbie pulled a manila folder from the satchel she'd been carrying. "You know, the kids help pick out their Absolutely Mom." Emily's heart soared. Abbie must know that Greg, Lisa and Bethany had selected her for a reason. The kids had asked for her!

The envelope Abbie handed her just said, "To Emily from Lisa." Emily opened it and, when she did, she understood why Lisa had sent it to her. On the small poster, a monkey was swinging through some exotic tree. The caption read, "Find a place you like and go there."

Emily grinned at Abbie. The gift was perfect. Of course she would go. She and Lisa could spend hours talking. And maybe someday Emily could gather enough courage to tell Lisa about her own mother. And then there was Greg, lanky and friendly, and little Bethany who had been so interested in her stories about Baby Sprout. Emily found she didn't care that much about the adult Mannings anymore. Not Clint or Philip or Amanda. She only wanted to be with the children and give them what she could—her friendship and her love.

When Emily had peeked into the locked cabin before, she hadn't been intrigued by its furnishings at all. She'd seen only a typical one-room camp house with two metal beds and a rustic kitchen, with a woodstove in the middle to keep everything warm.

Now, as she stood on the front porch with her suitcase in her hand, she saw that the cabin had been transformed. The kitchen was polished and spotless. A Kerr jar full of Texas flora that colored in the fall, pyracantha berries and yellow and red oak and maple leaves, waited on the ledge. It was such a simple, homey gesture that Emily couldn't help but be pleased. As Emily sniffed the wild weedy fragrance, she realized her priorities must already be changing, recalling the elaborate floral arrangements Lloyd always sent her after a particularly successful creative session.

The two metal beds had been replaced with an antique white wrought-iron bed, spread with a peach-colored coverlet. A fat, obviously loved, stuffed dog sat jauntily between the pillows.

"We didn't have any fancy furniture or anything," Lisa explained from the door where she stood. She had followed Emily around for the past forty-five minutes, ever since Emily and Abbie had arrived at the farm. "Bethany donated the dog. His name's Fluffy." She hesitated for a moment. "He's really her favorite animal, so you might want to give him back."

Emily was touched by the way Lisa cared for her younger sister. She picked Fluffy up and examined him. "It's good to have him here as a welcome. I'll return him to the house tomorrow."

As Emily glanced once more around the cabin, she realized that at this moment she couldn't imagine herself in any other place in the world. She was as happy as she could remember, surrounded by soft colors and the sun outside and the rustling of the trees. She wondered how long she would be living there, how long she would be part of this family. For one moment, she let herself wish it might be forever. But no sense wishing for something that would never be fulfilled. When Amanda came out of the coma, these children wouldn't need her around anymore. They would have their real mother back. And Emily wanted that for them as much as she wanted a family to call her own.

Emily's first morning at the farm, she awoke to a silence that seemed to be summoning her. She lay still, wrapped like a cocoon in the coverlet, listening. For a long moment she couldn't remember where she was.

The cabin. The pecan grove.

She didn't have to hurry. Clint Manning had told her she ought to take time for herself today, to get settled in. The family didn't expect her at the main house until much later.

When Emily closed her eyes again, she realized what she'd first taken for silence wasn't soundlessness at all. A meadowlark warbled from a distant cotton field. The trees outside whispered to her in bursts of breeze. Somewhere over the hill, a tractor chugged to life and a farmer started his day's labor.

Emily's heart pounded. Now that the time had

come to change her life, her nerves felt as taut as banjo strings.

I could be happy here, she thought. *I could.* But would she be able to help the children adjust to life without a mother?

Around her, the beauty of the grove seemed to reassure her, to murmur, "Don't be afraid. You can do this."

And Emily's heart responded in return, "Thank you. Thank you." Only she didn't have any idea to whom she was extending gratitude.

Emily certainly hadn't realized she'd be such a wreck now that the time had come to reach out to the children. She'd befriended them so easily before when she'd been here with Philip.

With her pulse racing, she trailed Clint Manning as he gave her a cursory tour of the house. He pointed out the pantry in the huge farmhouse kitchen and showed her the cabinet where Amanda kept the dishes. He gestured in the direction of the bathroom and his study and the screened-in back porch. He showed her the banistered staircase leading to the bedrooms upstairs. It all felt very formal this time.

Once Clint had outlined the family's schedule, Emily parked herself in the living room, her nerves jangling, and worked on a needlepoint until

Greg and Lisa and Bethany came in from school. It terrified her that the kids might seem hesitant to open up to her.

But Emily needn't have worried. She returned the stuffed dog to Bethany the minute the youngest Manning arrived home, and Bethany shyly asked her if she would like to learn how to sign the alphabet. Greg shot her a grin as he dumped what sounded like a thousand-pound backpack beside the front door and headed straight to the kitchen to forage for food. Lisa carried in a pottery bowl she had made in art class and gave a long account of the problems she'd encountered glazing it before she, too, made her way to the kitchen.

Emily marveled at how they accepted her presence. It seemed like no time at all before Emily found herself in the kitchen, too, supervising water in the microwave for hot cocoa and, horror of horrors, limiting Greg to eating only half of the pound bag of Oreos. He poured a massive glass of milk after he put the cookies away, then turned on the computer to check his "MySpace."

Not until a quiet evening several days later did Emily get brave enough to bring out the "Baby Sprout and Priscilla" manuscript. Then, carefully, so she wouldn't make many mistakes, Emily slowly read the story aloud to Bethany signing the alphabet the way she had learned.

But, at the same time, Lisa, Greg and Clint seemed to be having a shouting match in the study. Clint had been to visit Amanda before five that morning, and he was exhausted. He had come home to find that Greg had taken the Studebaker out of the garage and driven it to school. Lisa was involved because she was walking home with Tracy for the first time in many months, and Greg had given them both a ride into town to the Dairy Queen. Clint sounded angry with them all.

"What do you think I should do about this?" Clint asked his son in frustration. "I'd be open to any of your suggestions, Greg. You don't have a driver's license. Who do you think would have been responsible for your sister and her friend if you had had an accident?"

"I would have been responsible, Dad," Greg argued. "If I had gotten caught, I would have taken the blame. You don't have to treat me like I'm such a *loser.*"

"What if you'd gone off the road or something? Did you think about that?"

Emily couldn't help overhearing. She knew he probably intended to keep his voice low so he wouldn't scare his new employee to death during her first week here. But he wasn't doing a very good job of it. Emily was doing her best to distract the little girl. Bethany was reading the manuscript aloud now. They were sitting beside the fire, heads together, laughing and reading, when Emily heard whistling outside and someone tromped across the wooden porch.

"Anybody home?" The screen door swung open. There stood Philip Manning at the door with an overnight bag on one arm.

Emily grabbed Bethany's arm without thinking. Now she felt silly, for Clint had told her that Philip wandered in and out whenever he pleased. She had been expecting to see him but, even so, she wasn't prepared. Even though she'd mulled it over, she hadn't decided what she wanted to say when she saw him. She certainly hadn't imagined his wandering in and finding her sitting on the floor in his brother's home. Emily thought he looked like someone had pulled the rug out from under him. He looked betrayed, as if he thought she had set up an elaborate scheme to double-cross him.

"Hello, Philip," she said quietly as Bethany stopped reading in midsentence. Emily could have smacked herself, because her voice sounded so timid. She was desperately glad to see him, but she was uncertain how he'd respond. She had a horrible feeling just then when she saw the look on his face, the feeling that she wasn't good enough for any of them, that she had nothing to give the children, that she should never have come. It was a flashback to her own childhood, into the hundreds of days when her mother had walked into the room and had looked down at her with dizzy distaste.

"What are you doing here?" he asked in a neutral tone that sliced Emily's heart.

Bethany piped up, "She's our new adopted mom," saving Emily from a lengthy explanation. The nine-year-old tilted her head and smiled at her uncle. Emily was still holding her arm. "She's helping us until Mom gets well."

"I see." Philip's voice was sharp-edged as he eyed her. "I certainly didn't expect to see you here."

"I know," she answered, and as she did, she felt as if she'd unintentionally played a cruel joke on him by being here. She'd thought only of herself. Until this moment, she hadn't realized what it would look like to him.

"Where's my brother?" Philip asked. Emily wanted to shout at him. He had brought her here before and had played a nice game with her, but when it came to sharing what really mattered—his family—she could see he didn't want to do it. He made her feel the way her mother used to make her feel—guilty and sad and *wrong*.

"He's in his study with Lisa and Greg," she almost snapped, and even as she said the words, she was mad at herself for her tone of voice. She was feeling possessive and defensive, as if he was the outsider, not her. Philip pushed open Clint's study door and Emily heard the conversation inside halt.

Emily stared at the wall, a sick feeling in the pit of her stomach, until Bethany interrupted her. "Are you unhappy? What's wrong?"

"Oh, Bethany—" Emily shook her head as she turned toward the girl "—I'm fine. Just tired, I guess. I think I'd better go to bed."

"Can we finish reading later?" Bethany asked. "I like your story."

"Sure. Of course we can. Just not now."

Emily gathered her things and plodded along the path through the dark meadow. She sat in the little cottage for a long while, with the lights off, wondering about Philip, if he would talk Clint into sending her away, if this cabin would still be her home tomorrow.

The lights in the main house stayed blazing until long after midnight. Philip perched on the corner of his brother's desk, his feet planted angrily on the floor, his arms crossed, feeling grim, while Clint grounded Greg from even looking at the Studebaker for a month. Philip remained in a foul temper and silent while his brother held out a hand for Lisa's cell phone and informed her that it might be another decade before she earned the right to use it again.

Lisa wailed, "How can you do that to me, Daddy? It was *Greg* driving!"

With defeat in his eyes, Clint watched them both go.

Philip might have had mercy on his brother any other day; Clint looked every bit as morose and subdued as the two teenagers that had just sulked from the room. But Emily's presence on the farm irked Philip too much for him to let it go. "Well," he said, his arms tightening across his chest as he stood. "You told me you'd decided to go ahead with the 'Absolutely Mom' thing. Guess you forgot to mention the fact that you'd hired a woman I know."

"What's with you?" Clint shot back. "What? You going to attack the way I run my life, too?"

"I'm not attacking your life."

"What else would you call it?" Clint scrubbed his temples in frustration. "When you come into my house and tell me what you think I ought to do?"

Philip shrugged.

"You're the one who convinced me to hire someone in the first place. Or maybe you don't remember that. And maybe you don't remember that I asked you how well you knew Emily last week. You said you didn't intend to see her again."

"That's just *it.* I didn't intend to see her again. What's she doing here?"

"Your friend Abbie Carson thought she would be right for the job. And so did the children."

Philip said, "So Abbie Carson is in on this little joke, too."

"Dude, it isn't a joke." Clint could remember only weeks before when Philip had practically begged him to call Absolutely Moms and hire someone. Now, ironically, he had done it and Philip was mad. "We all like Emily. And Lisa loves her. The two of them have become friends. And Lisa is making friends at school again because of her."

Philip shook his head in frustration.

"I thought you wanted what was best for my kids, bro. I've been waiting until the right time to tell you I hired Emily. In case you haven't noticed, my hands have been full. And we're all starting to really like her."

"You keep telling me how careful you and Amanda are to mirror your faith in front of the kids. You don't even know where this girl *stands*. You can't just hire anybody who shows up on your doorstep."

"Give the woman some credit, Philip. I have a feeling about this. She applied for the job. Abbie brought out information on several women she thought would be appropriate. We picked Emily."

Silence.

"You're attracted to her, aren't you? I haven't seen you act this way about anyone since you worked with Morgan Brockner."

Philip raked his fingers through his hair. "Of course I'm not," he lied.

Clint called his bluff. "Then I don't see where we've got a problem then."

"I walk in and find her sitting on the living room floor. She looks up at me like she belongs more to this family than I do."

"Could be—" Clint reached to turn the lamp on "—that she reminds you of something you don't trust yourself to have. Something you don't trust God to let you have. Something you don't think you're good enough for."

An eighteen-wheeler rumbled past in the distance. Breeze fretted the leaves in the trees. Philip shoved his hands in his pockets and stared out the window into the darkness.

"Did that ever occur to you?"

"You're way off base, Clint."

"I don't think so."

"What do you know about my life?"

"I know you'd have every reason in the world to back away from a woman. I know how Morgan used you."

Philip faced his brother. "That's ancient history. I'm stronger than that." And his brother had no idea about his second relationship with Erin, his prayers, Erin's easy decision to leave him behind and become a missionary overseas.

"Are you?"

"Yes."

"I don't know that I would be that strong."

"You'd be stronger than you think."

"Than I *think?* You want to know what I *think?* I think that every time you feel like you want to fight for a woman, you run in the other direction because you don't want to fail at being what she needs you to be."

It took every ounce of control Philip could muster not to grab up his bag and head for the door. *I don't need this.*

"I think you've gotten real good at hiding behind the closed doors in your life. I think you've gotten real good at blaming those closed doors on God."

Philip began to yank open the buckles on his overnight bag. His fingers shook from the effort of controlling his anger. Who did Clint think he was, talking to him about failure? How could Clint talk about closed doors when his wife lay in a coma and no one knew if she would come out of it or not?

This is my family, too, and I'm not going to give up my place in it. With firm conviction, Philip pulled an extra pillow and a couple of extra blankets off the top shelf of the closet. He marched to the bedroom Amanda kept set up for him, pitched the extra decorative pillows aside and straightened the blanket on the bed as if he were laying claim to some formidable territory. *This is my domain and I'm not giving it up, I don't care who Clint has hired to take care of his household.*

Long into the night, Philip lay staring at the ceiling. Long into the night, Philip wrestled with his brother's words. *You have every reason in the world. You don't want to fail. You don't trust God.*

Emily had said, *If you're one of those church-going types, I don't want anything to do with it.*

Long into the night Philip prayed, *Father, will You show me what to do?*

Chapter Seven

Emily couldn't stop shivering the next morning when she awoke; the cabin was freezing and something inside her felt icy, too. She didn't know where she would go if Philip made her leave. She had already subleased her apartment for the next six months, and she didn't dare go back to Lloyd and tell him that she had been wrong.

In the past few days, she had given everything she had to give to Clint and the children. Seeing Philip last night had defeated her.

Emily walked to the main house to start cooking breakfast, and she was relieved to find the kids still asleep. It was Saturday and Clint hadn't yet gone to see Amanda. Philip was upstairs showering, Clint told her.

Emily was mixing batter for apple-raisin muffins when the telephone rang and she heard Clint answer it. He motioned for her. "The call's for you, Emily."

"Who is it?"

"She didn't say."

Emily took the call in his study, and when the woman on the other end of the line started talking, her voice sounded so feeble that Emily almost didn't recognize it. "Mother?"

"Yes." The voice haunted her from a distant past. She barely noticed Clint grabbing a folder of papers from the file cabinet and waving goodbye to her before he visited his wife. Emily held on to a chair for support. Her knuckles whitened, she clenched it so tightly. "I stopped by your office to see you in Dallas the other day and you weren't there. They gave me this number. Where on earth are you?"

"Here," Emily said, badly shaken. It had been a long time since she had talked to her mother, or wanted to. "On a farm. In Waxahachie." As Emily spoke, she didn't see Philip come down the stairs behind her and head for the kitchen. He'd showered and shaved and he needed a refill of coffee. Once he was in the kitchen, Philip couldn't help but overhear. Emily's voice was quiet, but it was shrill and quavery, too, and her words easily carried into the next room. "I'm working here."

"Lloyd Masterson tells me that you're babysitting children." The voice on the end of the line oozed polite displeasure. It was a tone of voice that Emily had grown accustomed to over the years. "And you've quit that wonderful position at the advertising agency. You know that's what we sent you to college for. You wanted to be a professional."

Emily flinched. Her mother had not sent her to college. Her father had. And Emily had helped him. The money she had earned during an internship with a local newspaper had gone to pay for books and part of her tuition each semester. "I still am a professional." It was all she could say right then. Tears welled up in her eyes, and her knees felt like they would buckle.

"I went by to see you so we could go to lunch together. But no luck." Her mother could even make her feel guilty about that.

"Where are you, Mother?" Emily asked. "The last time I talked to Daddy, he had no idea where you lived."

"I live in Dallas," the woman said, her voice disarmingly pleasant. Emily had no way of knowing if her mother was trembling, too, on her end of the phone. "I should call your father, I suppose." Then she added, "Does he know about this new endeavor of yours?"

"Of course, Mother." Emily took a deep breath. "I'm proud of what I'm doing. Daddy promised he'd come out and visit the farm sometime to see it. I'm living here taking care of three children who've lost their mother." She didn't add, *just as I lost mine.* For if she acknowledged the things she was thinking just then, she was certain that she would lose control and rage at the woman or simply start to cry. She couldn't do either. Not here. Not now.

"Why didn't they just hire a babysitter? I was proud of you when you were an advertising executive. I enjoyed talking about you to all my friends."

"You can still do that, you know," Emily reminded her.

"What am I going to tell them now? That you live on some man's farm and you're babysitting his kids?"

Emily couldn't endure the conversation much longer. The job with Clint and the kids was beginning to mean a great deal to her, and her mother was belittling it. They hadn't talked to each other in months, and even now her mother couldn't do anything except criticize her. Emily's heart ached. "I don't care what you tell them, Mother." But as her mother's disapproving voice droned on, Emily wondered if maybe she had made the wrong decision. Philip seemed to think so. "You've got to try to understand," she pleaded as if she wanted to convince herself as well as the woman on the other end of the telephone line. "I need this. I need to know I can love someone, that I can nurture others, that I can be a whole person, without having you and your alcoholic friends around to approve or disapprove." It was a cruel thing to say and Emily knew it. "Please, Mother, don't make me feel guilty about this, too."

"When have I ever made you feel guilty about anything?" The two had lived together for eighteen years and they didn't know each other at all.

Emily said something that had been swimming in her head ever since she had met Abbie Carson. "It's people who are important, Mother. Don't worry about things or reputations." She suspected that one of the reasons her mother had turned to alcohol a long time ago was that she was concerned about her own reputation and the things she owned. "When it comes down to the bottom line, it's the people in your life who matter, not the awards you've won or your bank account or your professional image. People are all the same, Mother. And life is so much easier if you like them."

"You're being totally disrespectful." There were muffled noises on the other end of the line, and Emily couldn't tell whether she was sobbing or just angry.

"I'm not being disrespectful. I'm telling you something you need to know." She could have added, *because I love you,* but she didn't. She wasn't certain whether she loved her mother. She didn't know if she was capable of it now. She had once, but that had been a long, long time ago. That was the worst thing of all, she had loved her mother, and her mother had made her feel like she wasn't worth much. Emily was about to say something else, to try to make amends, but she realized it was too late. Halfway through her next sentence, Emily heard a dial tone. Her mother had hung up on her.

Emily stared at the buttons on the telephone until they became a blur. She listened to the harsh tone as an immense wave of homesickness washed over her. When Philip went to her, he found her sobbing with the telephone receiver still in hand.

"Emily," he said, his voice gentle. He knew he had overheard something very private and very important. Whatever Emily's mother had said had shattered her. He had no way to know that it hadn't just been today's call that had done it. It had been a lifetime of pain and rejection.

The tears streamed down Emily's face, and Philip couldn't help but compare her to a Raggedy Ann doll, with no makeup and flushed cheeks, dressed in blue jeans and a red plaid flannel shirt, looking totally broken. Philip was suddenly very, very sorry for the things he had said to Emily last night.

"You're here because of her, aren't you?" he asked.

She nodded. "I guess I just had to get away from all that."

"The fighting with your mother?"

"I haven't seen her in a long time, Philip," she said. "Remember when I told you..." She paused. She was about to tell him something that had been very hard to tell anybody. But the events of the morning had broken down her reserve. "...that my mother had been sick once? She's an alcoholic, Philip. I haven't really had a mother, ever."

He took the receiver from her and placed it in its cradle.

"When I talked to Abbie and she told me about Absolutely Moms, it seemed like her ideas and this chance to be a mother for somebody might help me resolve all of it—" She stopped.

"You told her the right things, you know. You

told her that it was people who counted, not jobs or images or awards." How different his own life might have been if he and Morgan had only been so wise. "Maybe someday she'll realize that."

"I'm sorry, Philip." Emily expected him to tell her he wanted her to leave now, but he didn't. "I shouldn't have just come to your family like this. I should have called to let you know, at least. I'm certain that you and Clint and Abbie can find someone who will be a better adopted mom for the kids."

"Emily, I'm not going to be selfish enough to ask you to leave them. Clint told me last night that my nieces and nephew are growing fond of you. I wouldn't take that away from them. No matter what I want—"

He didn't need to finish the sentence for her to know what he didn't dare say.

I want you to go. I don't want you around people I care about.

They heard Bethany coming downstairs, and Emily's back straightened as she dried her eyes and hurried to the kitchen to pour muffin batter into the tins.

"Jumping Jehoshaphat," Philip signed to Bethany when she came romping into the kitchen. "Good morning."

After that, Emily's first Saturday on the Manning farm was a special one. Clint remained at the hospital most of the morning, but the rest of them strolled out into the pasture and spent the day meeting the cows. Greg was strangely quiet but he went with them, too, and Emily was honored to have so many people showing her around.

There was one particularly friendly cow that followed them across the pasture, and after following them a good while, the animal nosed Emily.

"That cow is Honey Snookems." Bethany held Emily's hand. Excited, she stopped walking and broke her grasp, to sign *Snookems* for her. "Her mama died when she was little so we had to feed her from a bottle, and now she follows us around."

"She's just a stupid cow," Greg said to Emily.

As the morning drew to a close, the boy went back to the house to hide behind the computer again.

"He's certainly in a mood today," Philip commented.

"It's because he got grounded from the car." Bethany's eyes were somber. It sounded like the ultimate punishment to her. "Dad says he can't even work on it. He's just bummed because he doesn't have anything to do."

"I think it's more than that," Emily said quietly, after Bethany had run on ahead.

Philip agreed with her. "He's not the kind of kid who holds a grudge. He outgrew that in junior high school. I wonder what's eating away at him?"

"I think he needs to see his mother." Emily stared straight ahead at the meadow where they were walking. She had been here less than a week and she didn't know if she should offer her opinion. She offered it to Philip, knowing she couldn't make things any worse between them than they already were. "He told me his father had never let him go to the hospital."

"Maybe so. Maybe you're right."

"What can I do? How can I say anything to Clint?" she asked him.

"You might have to wait a little while."

"I guess I will," she agreed with him. "I hate to come here and start giving my opinion when it isn't asked for." But she was right about Greg. It was time Clint let all the children visit their mother. He wasn't protecting them any longer. By keeping them from their mother, Emily suspected he was feeding their fears.

Lisa had gone back to the house earlier, and Emily and Philip were alone except for Bethany. She skipped toward them from across the pasture, and together the three of them walked back to the house. It would never do to let the children feel the tension between them. Philip swung Bethany up onto his shoulders and he gave her a piggyback ride as she laughed and whooped and Emily walked quietly along beside them.

When they arrived back at the house, Clint was sitting in his easy chair trying to concentrate on the newspaper, but it was clear to Emily that he was exhausted. She knew immediately that it had been his visit with Amanda that had drained him so.

Emily cast a knowing glance at Philip as the three girls headed toward the kitchen to make pizza for lunch. Greg was upstairs in his room, and Emily knew just by watching him that Philip was concerned about both his nephew and his brother. A few minutes later, Philip came into the kitchen and offered to slice pepperoni. Emily waited until the girls had gone out to set the table before she said anything. "He's exhausted, isn't he?"

"I don't know how much longer he can keep this up." Philip's voice was low. "He and I may have had our differences this weekend. But he's my baby brother. I hate to see him this way."

"You can't do anything for him, Philip." Emily took a handful of the pepperoni pieces and began laying them evenly on the pizza she was preparing. "You have to just love him, I guess. He'll draw the strength he needs from that. It's the only thing you can do. Someday things will change." Amanda could wake up tonight, Emily thought. Or she could be gone, too. Whatever the outcome, the situation couldn't be harder for anyone to deal with. Anything seemed better than this nagging uncertainty. "It would help if Clint would let the rest of the family share a part of the burden. He's a good father, but he's forgetting that two of his kids are almost adults."

After lunch, Philip pulled a wooden case full of watercolors and a paintbrush from under his bed and he stayed in his porch room sketching the scene behind the house. He had a picturesque view of the blacklands with Clint's rickety, homemade grape arbor in the foreground. This was one of Philip's favorite things, drawing on the farm, where the world around him was full of freedom and peace. He kept an extra set of paints here at all times. He knew himself well enough to know that he did his best work when he was inspired. And here, at the place where he had watched his nieces and nephew grow, where he had watched his brother build a love and a life, was where Philip often found himself the most moved to create, to sketch, to see.

"What are you doing all holed up in here by

yourself?" came a timid voice from the doorway, and he turned to see Emily leaning against the jamb. She stood there, looking so tentative, as if she wasn't certain she should be disturbing him. "Am I bothering you?"

"No." He shook his head. He'd decided while he was painting that they owed it to his family to call a truce between them. After lunch, Clint had hurried to Waxahachie to show several properties to a client. Lisa and Bethany had gone with him to have a soda and meet friends at the movie theater. Philip had decided Emily probably wanted time to herself this afternoon, too, after her heartrending conversation with her mother this morning on the telephone.

Philip was glad that she had come back to the house. He was worried about her and about the things her mother might have said to hurt her. There were so many things Philip understood now about Emily that he hadn't been able to understand before. He looked at her today and saw her in a different light. And he wondered if the feelings she ran away from, the things he knew she felt when he dared to touch her, might bring back some distorted memory of pain as she had known it long ago.

Is this what You're doing, Lord? Did You bring her to this place to heal her?

He motioned to her. "Come on in."

Clint was wrong about me trusting You, Father. I do trust You. But maybe I've been trusting You for the wrong thing.

"So this is where you stay when you spend your weekends on the farm?" She spun around and took in the details of the room. It was just as homey as her tiny cabin was, only without the extra feminine touches. The single bed in the corner had a massive hand-carved headboard made of oak, and it was covered with a patchwork quilt that sported squares of reds, blues and yellows.

"It's nice, isn't it?" he asked her. "This is my place. Manderly set it up for me a long time ago."

"Do you paint much when you come here?" She nodded her head toward the watercolor he was working on. He had just completed drawing in the grape arbor, and he was preparing to paint the hills a bright green where they spanned the horizon.

"All the time." He was making rapid strokes with his brush as he talked to her. "I keep this set around just in case I get inspired." He cocked his head and smiled across the room at her. "And that happens pretty often out here."

"You know You're shirking your job, don't you?" she asked him. He stared at her. Philip wasn't certain what Emily was talking about.

She was still leaning against the doorjamb with

her arms crossed and grinning down at him. "You promised me you'd work on the storyboards for my book. I haven't seen you doing any Baby Sprout sketches lately."

"I didn't know if you wanted me to work on those anymore," he said to her.

Father? Are You using this to open a door between us? So I can talk to her about You?

Emily bit her lip and leaned her head back against the wall.

"I wish you had told me from the beginning," he said.

"Told you what?"

"About your mother."

"That she was an alcoholic?"

"Yes."

"Well, what difference would it have made? Stuff like that happens to everybody."

"I'd like to draw your pictures for you, Emily." He picked up his sketchbook and leafed through it. He knew, even as he pressed her for this, that it was a big step for him to mean this, after what he'd been through with Morgan.

"I learned at the agency how hard it was to take a conceptual idea and turn it over to another person. I'd already pictured in my mind what I wanted and it was hard to turn it over to a professional artist."

Philip flipped another page in his tablet. "That's one reason I chose not to become a professional artist. I don't handle frustration well."

Emily shook her head. "You can say that again."

He didn't answer. He just looked at her with a disgruntled expression. Then he couldn't resist grinning. "You are a frustrating woman."

Emily pulled a copy of her manuscript from behind her back. "We can have a lawyer draw up some sort of contract, if you'd like. I'll give you a percentage of my first three million sales. How does that sound?"

"Let me take a look at that manuscript," he said as he took it in hand. "You can just owe me half your book advance and five percent of the royalties."

"Hey," she teased. "You sound like you know what you are talking about."

Philip took stock of the manuscript and began to read. Emily stared out through the screen while he turned the pages. The winter wheat was just beginning to pierce the ground, and Emily marveled at the rich growth that was covering the land so late in the season. The leaves clinging to the arbor covered the clusters of grapes like protecting hands.

It had been a stretch for Emily to let Bethany read the book, but it had been such a natural thing to do because the child had been interested and the two of them had been working at becoming friends. Philip's reading the manuscript was a different story altogether. He was a grown-up who would read her work from a grown-up's perspective. And even though Emily's story was written for a child in the third or fourth grade, there was a deeper meaning to her work, a message, that was likely to speak to Philip, too. She worried that he might think she was silly or crazy or both.

Philip flipped over the last page, and Emily was surprised when he looked up and she saw admiration in his eyes. "Emily." He whispered her name, and she didn't quite understand the respect in his voice. "You've got something here. Really. You send this thing in, and I'll bet you're going to find a publisher."

"Sometimes I don't think it matters, having it come out like that. What matters is that I've written it, that I've gotten the story out."

Philip held her manuscript out and tapped it with his index finger. "Your writing is very visual, Emily. I can picture this. Where is it?" He was thumbing through her work, trying to find a specific scene he thought he could illustrate well. When he found it, he sat in the chair again and pulled a drafting table out from the wall beside him.

Emily stooped beside him to see what he was doing. His fingers flew almost as fast as he was talking. "The scene in there where Baby Sprout first meets Priscilla," he said. "I think it's the third or fourth page." He made sharp, shading lines. "I need Priscilla's physical description." His pencil paused on the paper and he glanced up at Emily. "I guess you don't need to read it, though. You wrote it."

She found it hard at first. Emily quoted the lines from her work that said the nine-year-old girl had blond hair and that she was tall and willowy.

"Her eyes. What color are her eyes?"

"Brown," Emily answered.

"Like yours?" Philip looked down to where she was stooped below him and studied Emily's eyes.

"Darker than mine."

"Describe her face to me, Emily." Philip knew it had been sheer luck that he had drawn Baby Sprout so close to her expectations. He could have tried the same thing with Priscilla. But he wanted to be precise.

He finished eventually and held a rough sketch at arm's length so they both could see. "Does this look like Priscilla?"

"It does."

Philip instructed her, "Find the scene in there where Priscilla and Baby Sprout go to the old red sandstone courthouse to talk to old Judge Wyland. I like the part where she asks the judge if she can have a gold velvet throne to perch on in the middle of the town square."

"Here it is." Emily handed him her manuscript opened to the page he wanted.

Emily watched as he took his pencil in hand again and then drew the bottom half of a throne with twinkling lights on it. It was an avant-garde sort of drawing, with two chubby girlish legs that didn't quite touch the ground hanging down from the seat of the throne. Then, at the bottom of the page, he began to draw a close-up of Priscilla's face as she stared at the base of the throne above her. Philip drew the sketch so the reader would know that she was only picturing the throne in a daydream above her head.

"Does this look right?"

"Yes." She laid a tentative hand on his arm. "Maybe someday this will be a book."

"Someday may not be all that far away." He laid his hand on hers.

Philip watched while Emily trailed her eyes down to his hand. Philip steeled himself for what he thought she would do next. He expected her to jerk her hand away. She didn't. Instead she trailed her eyes back up and looked at him wistfully, full in the face.

She turned her eyes up toward him and he saw

the expression there that he hated, that eternal sadness, that hint of profound insecurity he had grown so familiar with since he had known her.

"I've been betrayed before by someone I cared about, too." He said the words flippantly, as if the fact held no importance to him now. "I know about the fears that you might harbor. I don't want you to feel you have to worry every time you come near me."

"I need a friend. I haven't had many of them, Philip."

He said, "Is it so hard for you to trust people?"

Emily thought about his question for a moment before she answered. "I suppose so." Then, "Don't you understand? It's not about betrayal. It's about who I *am*."

"Too many people think that way."

"I don't remember a time when Mother was happy. I ought to have been able to do something to make her happy."

"You were a kid," Philip reminded her. "It wasn't your job. God wouldn't want you to bear that burden."

She couldn't stop her reaction at his mention of God. Anger burned. "Don't talk about God to me, Philip. If God cared about me, he would have done something. Don't ever bring it up."

But he *had* brought it up. He wasn't going to turn away from that now. "Why does faith make you angry, Emily?" A certainty welled up in him. He felt compelled to speak it. "You prayed when you were a girl, didn't you? You believed once. You wouldn't be so resentful otherwise."

"One minute Mother would tell me everything I did wrong. The next, she'd drink and she'd get mean. She just checked out on us. She didn't want to deal with it anymore."

Philip knew he might as well be speaking to himself about this one; about the times he indicted himself for trusting Morgan. "You can't blame yourself for that."

"This morning when she called, I wanted to say, 'I like it better when you drink, Mother, because then, at least, you leave me alone.' That's what I blame myself for."

"But you could turn to your *faith*—"

He'd made a mistake. Philip knew it the minute he saw the color rising in her cheeks, the minute her voice began to tremble. "Daddy took me to church every Sunday when I was little, did you know that? I'd look at the mothers there who dressed their daughters from the *Delia's* catalog and who took the time to drive them where they needed to go and mouthed the words to every song during the choir concert," Emily blurted. "My mother never would show up. She wouldn't come to any of my school programs, either. I prayed so many times for God to fix her, to make her be well, but he never helped her. Why should I trust a God like that?"

"Maybe that isn't God's fault, Emily. Maybe it's your mother's." *Father,* Philip thought. *I know You haven't called me to fall for someone who doesn't trust You.*

"Why should I trust a God who would let me ask over and over again but would never do anything about it?"

Father, Philip thought. *I know You haven't called me to love a woman who doesn't love You.* So why couldn't he stop thinking of her?

"Don't turn away from your faith because of that. He's the only one who can heal you, the only one who can make it any better now. Only Him. Only God."

"All I ever wanted, Philip, was to be good enough for Mother to love me. God had his chance, don't you think?"

Philip watched her and thought about the joy he'd seen her find in the little things—things like baking muffins for the Manning family, climbing trees with Lisa, signing the "Baby

Sprout" story to Bethany. "You can't hold yourself responsible for something that your mother chose to do. Maybe you can't hold God responsible, either."

"Stop offering excuses, Philip. I quit church altogether because I got sick of excuses."

"You make your own commitment. You decide you aren't responsible for the choices your mother made."

"Commitment." Emily didn't try to hide the irony in her voice. "That's the other thing I don't believe in. My mother and father made a commitment to each other. I'd like to know what happened to that."

"Emily." He walked toward her, stopped right near her. "Don't be that skeptical about life. Skepticism isn't a part of you."

"Love doesn't last."

"How can you say that?" He couldn't believe she felt that way, too. "Look around you. Look at Clint."

"I see Clint. He's lost the only love *he* had, too."

When Philip and Clint had been on the school playground together, it had happened just this way, too. Philip reserved the right to disparage his brother whenever he felt the urge. But let somebody else come along and mess with Clint, and there'd be hell to pay. Philip would be the big brother, his fists swinging with vigor, protecting the Manning family name.

"How dare you come to this house and talk like that?"

She stared at him.

"When you see my brother, you see a man who has loved his wife through everything. They've overcome so much in their marriage, almost everybody does. They've had their financial troubles and they've brought up three kids together. They've committed themselves to each other. And, with God's help, they've made it work."

"I… I'm sorry, Philip."

"If Clint isn't going to give up hope on his wife, then I'm not going to give up hope, either."

"I shouldn't have said—"

"You're right. You shouldn't have said it."

Emily couldn't speak.

Too much damage had been done. "You can strike out at me all you want, Emily. But you have no right to be here if you feel that way. Clint *believes.* I won't let you undermine the only thing giving my brother strength."

Late that night, after the children had gone to their rooms and Philip had driven back to Dallas, Emily sat on her bed in the cabin. She stared out toward the moon hanging high overhead, her spirits low. She felt exhausted and hollow and sad.

She'd come to the Manning farm because she longed for an adventure that would help the kids along the way. She knew full well that her words had been born from her own broken heart, a wound that wouldn't let her see anything but her own hurt. Still, her own hurt had been the only thing she'd been able to hold on to throughout her life. She didn't want to let go of it.

I don't want to leave. I don't. Too many good things have happened to me here.

The next morning, when Emily went inside to make breakfast for the children, she began to shiver the minute Clint entered the kitchen.

What had Philip told his brother about their conversation last night?

She waited for Clint to confront her. She waited for the scowl that would indicate he knew that she had demeaned his marriage. But, "Good morning," Clint said as he reached overhead to pull down his favorite coffee mug. He offered her the same welcoming smile he offered every morning. "Sleep well?"

"Not really," she admitted.

"That bed okay out there?"

"Yes, it's fine. Very comfortable, actually."

"We've got to keep you comfortable." Clint filled his mug from the coffeepot. "That's important. Why couldn't you sleep?"

"I don't know," she lied.

Clint poured cream and stirred it in. "I'm headed to the hospital. After that, I've got showings all morning. You going to be okay getting the kids off to school?"

"Of course," she answered, as relief flooded her. *Philip must not have shared their conversation with his brother. In spite of Philip's anger, he hadn't repeated her disparaging remarks.* Although he'd been furious, he'd protected her.

Clint slurped from his cup. "We'll see you this evening then."

"Yes." Then, "Don't forget. Greg has band practice late tonight. They're marching in the football game Friday."

"Good you reminded me. Thank you."

"It's hard to keep up with them, isn't it?"

Clint laughed. "You can say that again."

After Clint left the room, Emily stood with her head raised, listening to the Manning family come to life. Outside the window, sparrows twittered and hopped from branch to branch in the trees. Greg's alarm went off, and his favorite CD started playing. Emily heard water running in Lisa's bathroom, and Bethany appeared, her face still swollen with sleep, at the top of the stairs. And Emily thought how Philip's questions disconcerted her, how they made her see that she didn't trust God and she didn't much trust people, either. Even with the household coming to life around her, Emily suddenly felt very, very alone.

When Philip parked in front of his office that morning, he found himself still incensed at Emily's comments. Where he'd once thought her to be flippant and full of joie de vivre, he now understood that she used her energy to cover the wounds she carried.

What does she think she's doing, using my brother's house as a hideaway from herself?

Philip parked his car in front of his real estate company and cut the engine. His firm steps echoed in the marble foyer as he entered the building. The security guard greeted him, and the three secretaries each bade him good-morning. Here, at least, he knew he was in charge of things.

The gold letterhead bore his name. Outside, his logo could be easily read by the thousands of commuters zipping past on LBJ Freeway. He could pick up the phone and clinch three deals before noon.

Every time he walked in the front door, he felt a commanding sense of power. This was his domain.

Ron Langford, a sales associate, met him when the elevator door opened on the seventh floor. "Got a minute?" Ron asked. "We've got a conference scheduled in fifteen minutes. Ben Huff wanted me to let you know. Some problem that's come up with the Robertson deal."

Philip frowned and stopped walking. What glitch had come up in Clyde Robertson's sale? Ben Huff, the firm's corporate lawyer, didn't call casual meetings. Philip didn't like the sound of this at all.

Langford said carefully, "I think you ought to know. Morgan Brockner is here with her attorney, too."

Philip didn't entertain any false illusions. Everyone in his office knew the reasons behind the intense competition between his company and Brockner Associates. It was the sort of thing Philip had fought to keep private, but even after all these years, people talked.

At mention of Morgan's name, Philip clenched the handle of his briefcase tighter. It was the only physical reaction he had. "I'll be there," he said simply, his voice level.

Philip didn't hurry to the boardroom when the time came. Morgan would want him to hurry. She would be waiting for him to push open the door and begin accusing her. Well, let her wait. Instead he spent extra time in his office, pacing the floor, going over the Robertson file. And when he walked into the boardroom and faced her twenty minutes later, he kept his expression as hard and unreadable as cut granite.

"Well, Morgan," he commented as he shook her lawyer's hand. He didn't want this to last any longer than it had to. He wanted her out of his office. "What seems to be the problem?"

She smiled blandly and deferred to her attorney. "Scott Johnson is handling this. He'll fill you in on the details."

Philip's legal counsel, the gray-haired comrade named Ben Huff, looked decidedly worried. Philip tried to swallow the apprehension in his throat.

"Gentlemen," Scott Johnson said. "Please have a seat."

Everyone did, except for Philip, Ben and Morgan. Johnson waited for Morgan's signal. When she nodded, he carried on.

"We are gathered here to question the legality of the real estate transaction that is scheduled to close this afternoon, the transaction between Robertson, Inc. and Mike Spencer."

Philip's fists stayed clenched at his sides. *What will she think of next?* Absurd. Morgan had known about the Robertson deal closing for weeks. Why had she waited until the eleventh hour to bring a complaint?

As Scott Johnson spoke, it seemed he spoke about some other company, in some other place, his words sounding so foreign to the Manning sales associates in the room. A high-rise business complex Philip had listed for millions; the sales commission alone would keep the company going for a year.

But now Morgan's attorney was accusing him of forging documents to make himself eligible to sell the property. Scott Johnson insisted that Brockner Associates had been given an exclusive contract to sell the office complex on Dallas North Parkway. And then Philip almost choked when Johnson produced the papers to prove it.

Philip couldn't believe Morgan would stoop this low. He knew Clyde Robertson could shed some light on this misunderstanding, he thought, but the man was battling traffic on the expressway, trying to get here after one of those front secretaries had made a desperate telephone call.

Johnson's papers appeared perfect in every detail, right down to Clyde Robertson's familiar signature. Philip had been standing in the same room when Clyde had signed the exclusive contract with his company. A huge amount of money was at stake in this deal, but there was something much more valuable in question, too. Philip's reputation. It seemed Morgan Brockner was gunning for that, too.

Philip glared across the room at the woman whom he once had considered marrying. She stared back at him, her eyes as empty as cool glass. It sent ice through his veins, realizing she'd set out to ruin him. It didn't matter who he was or what they'd shared. He stood in her way. She would see him ruined.

"Morgan." He said the words in front of all of them. "Don't be a fool."

"You're the fool, Philip." Her tone was glacial and measured. "If you go through with the closing this afternoon, I'm afraid Brockner Associates will have to take you to court. And I can assure you, this won't play out well in the local media."

"Go ahead and take us to court," he exploded, and somewhere deep inside he knew that was just what Morgan wanted. "Your company name will be smeared across the Internet the same way you seem intent on smearing mine. You don't frighten me."

"Is that what you think I'm trying to do? You

think I'm trying to frighten you? I'm sure your legal counsel will advise you to hold off until we sort through this misunder—"

He didn't let her finish. "The closing will take place this afternoon at three. I doubt the general public will pay much attention to who's the plaintiff and who's the defendant in the drama. I worked for this sale. I earned it the same way I worked for this company. You won't take that away, Morgan. If you think you can, then go ahead and try."

"I will." She glanced pointedly at her lawyer, her eyes blazing to life as she stood to leave the room.

After she and Scott Johnson had gone, members of Philip's staff remained in the room, stunned and silent, waiting to see what might happen next. After a few beats Philip shook his head at them and shrugged. "I don't know," he said. "I just don't know."

Ben Huff stepped forward. Philip put up a hand to stop him. "I'll be in my office. Just let me know when Robertson gets in."

"I will," Ben promised.

Philip went to his office, shut the door wearily and buried his head in his hands.

Chapter Eight

Emily cooked breakfast for Clint the next morning before the sun even came up. She got the kids off to school, and during the day, except for planning meals, her time was her own.

Unable to get her mind off the words she'd exchanged with Philip, Emily donned her hat and set out into the pecan grove. With each step she took through the deep grass, she tried to escape from her mistakes and failures. With each step she took she counted her regrets.

How could I have compared my own hurts with Clint's life? He's never done anything to deserve what's happened to him.

By the time she reached the barbed-wire fence, Emily's heart throbbed with dull pain.

Why did Philip have to hear me saying those things to Mama?

Cotton had ripened in the fields, and everywhere Emily turned, the bolls had exploded open into acres of white fluff. To the north, she could see a cotton gin working. *Why did he talk to me about unanswered prayers? How did Philip even know to ask?* She stood among the rows of trees, listening. The wind in the leaves sounded like rain.

After she returned to the house, Emily rifled through the kitchen, searching for something to bake. She found overripe bananas and settled on banana bread. After she lined a suitable pan with wax paper, she whipped together flour, sugar, a dash of buttermilk until she liked the consistency of the batter. With every turn of the spoon, Emily convinced herself she had been wrong to come here. She hadn't been worthy of being loved when she was little. She certainly wasn't worthy to help this family now. Philip had made her see that.

Her tears fell unbidden. She couldn't stop them. She poured the batter into the pan and, in desperation, wiped her nose with the length of her sleeve.

Won't I ever be able to do anything right?

By the time the children arrived home, a loaf of golden-brown banana bread, still warm enough to melt butter, waited on the farmhouse table.

"Something smells really good!" Lisa said the minute she walked in the door. Bethany was right behind her.

"Come see." Emily wiped her eyes quickly. It would never do for the kids to see her upset. But she needn't have worried; the girls barely noticed her as they abandoned their backpacks and pulled paper plates out of the cabinet.

"Where's your brother?" Emily picked up their backpacks from the floor and set them in a chair.

Lisa shrugged.

"He was right behind us," Bethany said.

Emily peered out the window in search of Greg. "That's funny. Why didn't he come in?"

"How should I know?" Lisa said around her first bite of bread.

Emily waited until she'd filled the dishwasher and the girls were spreading their homework on the table before she went in search of Clint Manning's son. She'd salvaged a couple pieces of bread for him on a napkin; if she'd left it to the girls, they'd have left nothing but crumbs.

She didn't have to search hard to find Greg. When she swung open the door to the ancient barn-board garage, there he stood, working beneath the hood of the Studebaker. He didn't unfold himself or acknowledge her when she entered. She could tell by his firm stance and by the awkward jut of his elbows that he knew someone was watching.

"I brought you a snack," she said. "I know how you're always famished after school."

"Thanks, but I'm not hungry."

Oh, really. "You sure?"

"Yeah."

"Guess I'll take it back inside and let your sisters have it, then."

Greg disentangled himself from the innards of the car so he could have a look at what he might be missing. If Emily had to guess what grimy Studebaker part he was holding, she'd say it might be the steering column.

"Maybe I could eat something."

"Thought so." Then, "I'll leave it here." She set the napkin on a shelf where he could get it after he wiped his hands.

Greg waited for her to say something more. When she didn't, he asked, "You aren't going to tell Dad, are you?"

"What? That you're doing something you're not supposed to do? That you're working on your car?"

"Yeah."

"I'm standing here watching you, wondering if telling your dad is in my job description. You *are* grounded, Greg."

He laid the steering column on the ground among a large collection of other pieces he'd apparently dismantled. "I need time away from everybody. I need to sort through stuff. If Dad finds out, it's not going to matter one way or another anyway."

"Why won't it matter?"

"Midterms came out today."

Emily waited.

"Dad's going to kill me."

"Is he? Your grades went down?"

"That's sort of an understatement."

She sighed. "I think you ought to come in the house. It puts me in the middle, knowing you're out here."

Greg wiped his hands on a rag like he wanted to wipe his hands of his whole life. "That's not my problem. That you're in the middle."

"Greg."

"This isn't about you," he said. "In case you hadn't noticed."

"I'm not trying to corner you, Greg," she whispered before she left him alone. "You have to understand that."

"Why did you come out here looking for me, then?"

"Because I care about you."

"Right."

"You think you're not worth caring about?" she asked.

In answer to her words, Greg seized a wrench and dove under the hood again. Whatever his task, the wrench clanked so loudly that Emily couldn't get another word in edgewise.

"I'm headed to the house," she shouted, her heart heavy.

She thought she heard the muffled question, "So what's stopping you?" coming from the car.

Emily found the girls just finishing their homework. Clint would be home in an hour; she still hadn't decided what to do. The pounding sound of Greg's frustration rang in Emily's ears long after she'd closed the kitchen windows and had turned the television on.

That evening, every time a car went by on the highway, Emily lifted her head to listen. For all the harsh words they'd exchanged the last time they'd seen each other, Emily knew instinctively that Philip would be the one to give her much-needed advice about Greg. He came to the ranch often to visit his family; she hoped he would show up tonight.

Only, he didn't.

Each time a car passed Emily waited to hear the

crunch of gravel as it turned in across the cattle guard. But it never did. As supper dragged on, Greg hunkered at one end of the table while his father, oblivious, ate heartily at the other end. Emily glanced up often to find Greg watching her warily, expecting any minute for her to blurt out the truth to his father. *Your son is disobeying your wishes. He isn't following your rules.* But something stopped her. She ate silently, passing serving bowls whenever she noticed anyone needing anything, catching Greg's gaze whenever she had the chance, trying to reassure him.

By the time everyone's plates had been scraped clean, Greg's shoulders didn't slump quite so much. He didn't look ready to bolt. When they met each other in the hallway later that night, Greg stared down at her, astonished. "You didn't tell my dad."

"No. I didn't."

"Why not?"

She shrugged. "For the time being, we'll keep it between us. You and I both need time to figure out how to best handle this."

Greg hesitated. "I work on the car when I need to be by myself and think. It *helps* me, fixing the Studebaker. I have to be *alone*."

"I think I can understand that."

"He won't let us see her, you know. I haven't

talked to my mom since the morning before she went in for surgery."

"You ought to talk to him, Greg. You ought to tell your father what you need. That's your place, not mine."

When Philip didn't visit his family that night or the next night or the next, Emily blamed herself for his absence. Philip had made it clear he didn't respect the reasons she'd come to work for his brother. But Emily didn't have time to dwell on Philip's disapproval. As the days wore on and she watched Greg continue to defy his father, her concern for the boy overpowered everything else. When Clint received Greg's midterm grades in the mail, he took Greg to task in front of the girls. "Don't you know I'm trying as hard as I can to keep this family together?" Clint bellowed. "The least you can do is get your homework done. Do you think you can do that much? Do you?"

As the days passed, Emily wondered if she was the only one who noticed that Greg had stopped joining in at the dinner table. He never laughed at anything funny. Whenever one of the girls asked him a question, Greg jerked to attention, looking startled, as if he didn't think anyone knew he was there.

Finally, in desperation, Emily phoned to set up a coffee meeting in Dallas with Abbie Carson.

When Abbie answered the phone, she sounded delighted to hear news from the farm. And when Emily walked into the café, Abbie was already waiting, grinning, with a huge mug in front of her.

"I'm so glad to see you." Abbie rose and gripped Emily's hands. "I can't wait to hear how everything's going."

"Well, I've got some stories to tell you," Emily said. And after she'd ordered tea, she leaned forward and talked for a half hour about Lisa's friends at school and Bethany's latest art project and about Clint visiting the hospital every morning before his office opened.

"Sounds like the girls are doing great," Abbie said, nodding her head with pleasure.

"It's been so much fun."

"And you? How are you doing, Emily?"

"I'm okay," Emily answered, thinking fleetingly of Philip and quietly missing him. She did her best to put him out of her mind, knowing the time had come to focus solely on the children who had become her responsibility. "I'd be better if Greg was better."

"What's up with him?" And at the concern in Abbie's voice, Emily sensed she had found a true friend.

"I don't know what to do," she said after she'd

told Abbie about Greg's midterm grades and his sneaking out to work on the car. "He's not just being defiant. That's why I chose not to go to Clint. I think his problem goes much deeper than that."

Abbie sipped her coffee.

"I think he's really hurting."

"It's understandable, with his mother as sick as she is."

"Maybe I'm wrong, but I feel like his father is stealing some of the grief process from him. Clint doesn't want the kids to see their mother in a coma, so he won't let them visit the hospital. The girls don't seem to mind, but Greg is going deeper inside himself. He acts like he doesn't even feel like he's part of the family sometimes."

"Have *you* been able to talk to Greg about it? Would he be willing to talk to his dad if you were standing there beside him?"

"I don't want Clint to think I'm ganging up against him, siding with his children. I don't know how comfortable I'd feel with that." Then, "Oh, Abbie," Emily sighed, leaning forward. "Maybe I told Greg the wrong thing. I told him this needed to be between him and his father, no one else. But maybe I should have gone to Clint at the very first, then I wouldn't feel like I was hiding something."

"You feel caught in between them?"

Yes. She felt trapped between everyone's needs. Her first priority seemed to be the children. But she didn't know; she'd been hired to help Clint stay informed about his children's lives.

"Clint Manning has entrusted me with so much. Someone else might do a better job with them. I'm trying to do the best thing for Greg, and instead I'm failing them all."

Abbie cupped her mug in both hands and waited.

"If I didn't go back to the Mannings, you could find someone better, couldn't you? Someone who knows about children? Someone who could make better decisions than I can?"

"You don't think you're worthy of doing this job, Emily?"

"It scares me that they trust me the way they do."

"You seemed so certain when you came to me before."

"I know." Emily toyed with her spoon.

"Look at me." When Abbie captured her gaze, Emily had never seen such certainty in the woman's eyes before. "Did you stop to think how God puts a person in a position she knows she isn't capable of? Not to make her feel unsure of herself, but to make her know how much she can trust Him?"

Emily stared at the woman, unable to believe her ears. Yes, she knew Abbie represented a Christian organization. But why was it, every time Emily turned around, she kept hearing the same message?

"If God has a job for you and He's called you to do it, then I couldn't find anyone better."

"I don't want to leave them," Emily said, her voice choked with emotion. "I've started to care for them so much. I just keep thinking there would be someone who could be *better* for them. If there would be, I'd want to step aside."

"I won't stop until I've convinced you." Abbie set down her mug and gripped Emily's hand across the table. "You must go back to them. You must do it with victory in your heart."

"Victory in my heart?"

"The Heavenly Father is the only one who can make you see what you are truly worth. And He will."

Emily shook her head, still dubious.

"The Heavenly Father is the only one you can really depend on to guide you into the right choices. All you have to do is pray."

On the way out of the coffee shop, Emily passed a row of newspaper stands. She glanced at the *Dallas Morning News* headlines the same as always. Three steps later she froze, backed up, read the banner again.

Multi-Million Real Estate Transaction Headed for Courts.

And the kicker, Manning CEO Fights for Life Amid Allegations of Wrong-Doing.

She stared at the paper, unable to believe the words. Only days before, this man had been standing before her, telling her, *You make your own commitment, Emily. You decide you aren't responsible for other people's choices.*

Emily fumbled in her purse for coins to feed the machine. Her hands were shaking so badly she couldn't find her wallet. By the time she'd rounded up two quarters, several people had taken copies and there weren't many left.

She shook open the paper and scanned the lists of names, dates and buildings in question. Other than Philip, no one else's name sounded familiar. As she read the details, the case seemed ominous.

For long moments Emily stood in the front foyer of the café, wondering what she ought to do. She had a good hour before she needed to be at the house to greet the children. Suddenly she found herself yearning to go to him. Did she dare? Even as she asked the question she knew the answer.

The traffic flowed well on the freeway; she arrived at Philip's office office in record time.

Several of Philip's employees nodded greetings as she followed a secretary up the hallway. They must remember her from the seminar she'd given. Returning to this place made Emily feel like she'd slipped inside a different world. It hadn't been long since she'd made the marketing presentation here, yet she felt as though it had been an eternity ago.

Emily stood in the doorway to Philip's office, holding the article. He glanced at her in surprise. "This is why you haven't been out to the farm," she said.

"You shouldn't have come."

"I was in town. I...wanted to see you."

His eyes were unfathomable. "Did you? Would you have come if you hadn't read the front-page story? Or did you stop by just to remind me that I had failed?"

"Philip. I came because I *care*."

He looked exhausted and sick. "I don't need you to care right now. I need to work this out on my own."

She stepped inside, closed the door behind her and said nothing.

"It's all over the newspapers, isn't it?"

"Yes."

He looked totally beaten.

"You don't have to do this by yourself."

"No matter how I handle it—" he pitched a pencil in the air "—the nightmare isn't going away. Bennett Huff's already started coming up with our defense. But Clyde Robertson, the man I made at least fifteen million dollars richer by the sale of his office complex, has decided not to testify. He told Bennett he didn't want his name dragged through the mud."

"Philip, I'm so sorry."

"I won't be coming to the farm for a while. I have to solve this problem."

"You will. I have no doubt of that."

"At every turn, Morgan is out to prove that I'm incompetent. And maybe I am—I've let her get the best of me. Robertson must have been in her camp from the very beginning."

"Morgan?"

"Morgan Brockner." He said her name with great distaste. "The plaintiff."

Pieces of the puzzle began to fall together for Emily. "You're on a first-name basis with her, then?"

"Yes."

"Is that normal?"

"It's normal if you were engaged once."

For the first time, Emily began to understand the scope of Philip's pain. No wonder he found ways to protect himself from people. No wonder he'd stormed out of his brother's house, accusing her of undermining Clint. *How dare you come to this house and talk like that?* For the first time she understood the wound that her careless words had inflicted.

"So you're watching Clint's marriage and *you're* wondering if it has a chance of survival. You're wondering if love has any chance of surviving ever. Because of what happened with *her.* Because of what's *still* happening."

"No matter the success I have or how much I achieve with my business, she finds a way to undermine that. I fail every time I let my guard down."

"You aren't a failure. You didn't *let* it happen. Morgan manipulates it."

"I should have seen it coming."

"What happened to the man who told me I was wrong to blame myself? That God wouldn't want us to bear such a burden?"

"I'm not asking for your criticism."

"I'm not criticizing you. I'm repeating something I found hard to accept. But, seeing you, I'm starting to think there might be some truth to it. I think you ought to listen to your own words. Because maybe I should have listened, too."

"I'll handle this," he said. "I'll handle this on my own."

"What happened to the man who told me that

only one thing, only God, could help a person completely heal?"

"How can *anything* heal," he asked, "when it keeps getting opened up again?"

Emily didn't reply. When Philip raised his eyes to hers, she saw that he finally comprehended. Their lives paralleled; her wound from her mother kept getting opened, too.

"Maybe there's a purpose for it," she said carefully. "Maybe it happened so I could have a chance to *see.*"

For an instant she watched Philip consider the option. But his features turned hard; she knew he would deal with this his own way. "I failed because I relaxed my guard."

"Maybe that isn't such a bad thing, Philip."

Shaking his head, he said, "I'm not ever going to let it happen again."

Chapter Nine

In spite of Philip's absence, Emily found she was more excited than usual about Christmas. When she thought about it she realized that, this year, the holiday would be different than it had ever been before for her. Her mother made it clear that she had better things to do than while away an entire day with her daughter. Her brother would be with an old roommate. Her father was spending his few days away with a friend. He had invited Emily to join him there, but she had declined. She knew he was planning a few restful days hunting on his colleague's deer license. She would miss her father but she longed for an old-fashioned celebration, and Clint had invited her to take part in theirs.

As the days sped past, Emily kept herself busy

shopping for the Mannings. For Bethany she'd found a large stuffed purple cow that played "Home, Home on the Range" in a high tinkling melody that Emily knew Bethany could hear. For Lisa, she found a strand of silver beads. They were a bit extravagant but they would make the girl feel so special and so grown-up that they were well worth the money. She wasn't sure what to buy Greg and finally settled on a hooded sweatshirt with his favorite band's logo on the front.

Shopping for Clint proved more of a challenge. After sorting through what felt like hundreds of hangers, she found a maroon button-down shirt that he might like. It would match the suit she'd seen him wearing to work lately.

If Emily had once stopped to consider it while the preparations continued on, she would have realized that the Manning-family Christmas would include attending church. Festive lights sparkled across the highway. Christmas carols sounded from the car radios. Signs sprang up in front of churches everywhere. "Come Worship the King." But Emily had stopped trusting Jesus so many years ago. She'd prayed for him to make her mother well, to make her mother stop drinking, and that hadn't happened. *If God cared about me, He would have done something.* It felt much too painful, remembering what she'd once hoped for. She didn't even notice the religious trappings of the season anymore. Christmas was something you *shopped* for, nothing more.

Many times she heard Clint on the phone trying to convince his brother to join them for the holiday. Many times Clint hung up the telephone in frustration. "I don't like the way he's cut himself off from everybody," Clint growled one evening after he'd come in from hanging Christmas lights on the porch. "It isn't right, especially not this time of year."

Each time Clint expressed concern about his brother, Emily's heart ached for Clint, knowing he must be feeling the absence of his wife keenly. Many times Clint would begin to speak of Amanda, only to stop midsentence. And every time the door creaked open or a car bounced across the cattle guard, Emily caught herself checking to see if it might be Philip. She'd gotten used to him driving out for visits with his family. She hadn't realized, until he stopped dropping by, how desperately she missed him.

Lord, if You are a healing God the way Clint says You are, then maybe I could be some sort of help healing this family. I want so badly to matter to someone.

No matter how many times she stopped to listen at the door, Philip never stepped through.

No matter how many times Emily stood on the porch wishing Philip would come, as the holiday lights from distant houses began to take on a glow against the dusky Texas sky, the ache in her chest refused to go away.

Doesn't he know that if he lets Morgan steal this from him, too, then he's let her steal everything?

On the morning of Christmas Eve, Lisa and Bethany bounded downstairs to find her drawing faces on gingerbread men with powdered-sugar icing. Greg came down for breakfast, too, and he didn't say much, but Emily thought it might be because the two girls jabbered on about presents and surprises during the entire meal. They were so excited to be out of school, neither Emily nor Greg had a chance to get a word in edgewise.

"Where's Dad?" Greg asked finally after Lisa and Bethany had deserted the table to scope out the gifts under the tree for the umpteenth time.

"Probably at his office by now. He went in early to see your mom this morning. He wanted me to let you know he'll probably be home by noon."

Greg watched her hand as she dripped icing to make two eyes on the ginger cookie. "Mom always made those," he said in a hushed voice.

"I know. Your father told me."

Greg didn't move.

Shakily she drew the mouth on the cookie. She turned to the silent boy beside her. "I'm not trying to take her place, Greg. I hope you know that."

Greg turned his attention to loading his plate with a second helping of eggs. He said nothing. Emily walked over to him and laid her arm across his shoulders. She had no idea how to bring up the questions she knew she needed to ask him. Here he was, sitting at the table with the weight of the world on his shoulders, and it struck Emily how much he resembled his uncle. There were times he looked old beyond his years, and Emily longed to do something to help him.

"Greg," she admitted softly. "I know something's wrong. If you want to talk, I'll listen. I want you to know that."

"I don't need to talk about anything," Greg said. That's the last chance they had to exchange words before the doorbell rang and she heard Bethany shriek, "Grandma! Grandpa!" Amanda's parents had arrived.

The Manning farm stayed busy the rest of the day. Emily fixed lunch and Amanda's mother helped while Clint and Amanda's father visited in the front room by the tree. Amanda's parents were a study in human resiliency, Emily saw, willing to make Christmas nice for their grandchildren while their daughter lay mute and ill in a hospital bed.

"Will your brother be joining us this year?" Amanda's mother asked Clint.

Emily saw Clint shake his head sadly. "He's caught up in business. Won't let himself get away." Clint shrugged. "Or maybe we're just too much for him this year. He's been such a support through this ordeal. A person gives, and then he needs time away."

Even so, Emily didn't give up at first. She checked out the window a dozen times that day. It wasn't until five-thirty, when Clint bounded downstairs straightening his necktie, that she finally gave up hope. Philip wasn't coming.

Clint must have noticed the downtrodden expression on her face. "You're coming to church with us tonight, aren't you?"

Emily started. That had never been anything she'd considered. "I don't think so. This is your family gathering, Clint, not mine. I'll just—"

"You'll just...what? Sit here and wait for someone to get here who isn't coming?"

"Clint."

"I see it, Emily. You're beginning to care for my brother, aren't you?"

She couldn't answer. At the top of the stairs, Lisa banged on the bathroom door to move Greg out so she could get to the sink. Bethany appeared, wearing a holiday dress.

"We're your family this Christmas, too. We want you to join us."

Bethany agreed. "Please. You have to go with us, *please?*"

"You *have* to come with us," said a male voice from inside the washroom.

"Greg!" Lisa shouted. "I *need* to get in there!"

Amanda's father passed all of them on the way out to warm up the car. And Emily found that she yearned to be a part of their traditions, just this once, to fit in with the family she'd grown to care for. No one would recognize her tonight or hold her accountable for her faith.

She straightened to her full height and nodded at Clint.

"Okay," she conceded. "I'll go."

The pews at Parkside Baptist Church were already crowded when they arrived, but Clint found a spot in the center near the back where the Manning clan would fit. Greg seemed to be gravitating toward her tonight, as if the few words she'd spoken to him at breakfast had done some good, and Emily nodded at him as he stood aside to let her slip into the seat beside Lisa. Greg slid in beside her.

Memories flooded her as Emily glanced around the room. A massive cross hung behind the altar. It reminded Emily of the cross that had stood outside the door of the church she'd attended with her father.

She watched families filing up the aisles, nodding at friends, hugging one another. She saw children squirming in their seats, excited about what the next hours would bring. The lights in the church dimmed then, and Emily was lost to the world as the spotlight came on in the sanctuary and there stood five tiny angels wearing white choir robes and tinsel-lined cardboard wings.

From behind the altar, the narrator held up a Bible and announced that he was reading from the Book of Luke. "'For behold, I bring you good tidings of great joy, which shall be to all people. For unto you is born this day, in the city of David, a Savior, which is Christ the Lord.'"

The angels disappeared then and there were only shepherds in the scene, traveling long distances, following a star to a rickety stable not so different from the dilapidated stable that stood at one end of the corral in the pasture at home. There the shepherds found Mary and Joseph and the

Christ Child while the children's choir in the balcony sang "Away In a Manger," a song that reminded Emily of years past, of a little girl clutching her father's hand, knowing her Christmas was going to be different from the ones everyone else talked about.

The narrator continued, "And so it was that this simple scene with these few players, a man and a woman and a babe, three kings and several bedraggled shepherds changed the world."

It's all such a nice story, Emily thought. *If only it were true.*

Near the end of the service, the ushers handed out white candles to everyone, and as the choir proceeded along the aisle, still singing, the ushers moved from pew to pew, lighting the worshippers' candles. As Greg turned to her and touched his burning wick to hers, he smiled gratefully at her. Emily smiled back. How different it felt, attending a service with this large, deep-rooted family instead of with a father who admitted he couldn't be certain what they would find at home.

The thought hit Emily like a blow. In many ways Clint Manning and her father were alike. Their situations were similar. Only, Emily's mother had been given a choice. Amanda had no choice at all.

How could one man give his children so much

hope, while another let the pain drive his family apart?

What had made the difference?

Emily turned to Bethany, touched her burning wick to the little girl's candle. As the flame flared between them, Bethany lifted her eyes toward Emily. "I want to pray for Uncle Philip," Bethany whispered. "Will you pray with me?"

In that instant, Abbie Carson's words echoed inside Emily's head. *You are worth so much... the Heavenly Father...guide you into the right choices...all you have to do is pray.*

The sanctuary was beginning to be engulfed in a golden, moving glow. Emily's breath caught in her throat. This was something, as a child, she'd vowed she would never do again.

With her head down and her throat clogged, she suddenly heard a voice speak. It was as clear as if someone was sitting in the pew beside her.

There is nothing stronger than the prayer of a child.

Emily lifted her chin to see who had spoken. Everyone was silent in the church, focused on lighting candles and worshipping. No one anywhere was speaking. Could she somehow be hearing the voice of the Lord?

I'm not a child anymore, she wanted to argue.

Then she heard a second sentence. And she was not certain whether the words had been uttered out loud or whether they had only resounded in her head.

You will always be my child, beloved. I love you more than you can ever know.

Emily felt a tug on her arm. She glanced down to find Bethany still waiting for her answer. "Will you?" the little girl asked again.

Emily's heart pounded. "I will," she agreed.

While the sanctuary grew alive with candlelight, Bethany reached for Emily's free hand. Emily wondered if the child could feel her hand shaking. But, instead, Bethany only bowed her small head and whispered, "Dear Jesus, take care of Uncle Philip tonight, would You? He wants to be away from us but please don't let him be away from You."

Bethany paused as if she expected Emily to say something, too. But Emily's lips felt as thick as tires. She couldn't say a thing that made sense. After a lengthy silence, she finally managed, "Yes." And with the utterance of that one word, Emily broke a vow she'd held on to since she'd been a little girl. As she prayed for Philip, for the second time in her life, she prayed that someone she cared about would get better. And that night, as she walked out into the cold darkness, she felt an odd new sense of peace.

Once they arrived back home, the Manning family tackled the massive pile of presents that had accumulated beneath the Christmas tree. There were dozens of packages for the girls from their grandparents, a lip gloss and eye shadow and a poster for Lisa, hair barrettes and an American Girl doll outfit for Bethany. Greg opened his gift and gave a loud whoop when he pulled out a steering-wheel cover for the Studebaker and an application for a personalized license plate.

Amanda's mother handed Clint the next box to open. But just as he started to rip the paper, his head shot up. "Wait," Clint said. "Did you hear that?"

"What?" Greg asked.

"I thought I heard a car drive up."

For the second time that evening, Emily's heart shot to her throat. Could it be Philip? Each of them paused, listening. The cows were stirring; they were bawling across the distant hill. But the yard was silent until, suddenly, outside, a car door slammed.

Lisa signed to Bethany. Bethany flew to the door in a flash. The screen flung open and Philip stepped in with an armful of packages. The cold came in with him.

Although he still looked pale and downtrodden, his smile was festive enough. "Hey," he said, as if his arrival had no significance whatsoever. He dropped the boxes beneath the tree. "Somebody run out to the car and help me unload. The trunk is full of packages."

"Philip," Emily whispered.

"And you're the biggest gift of all," Clint said, wrapping his arms around his brother in a bear hug.

For a long moment Philip didn't respond to his brother's comment. He allowed the hug to last. Then, finally, he clapped his brother on the back. "A person needs family at a time like this." And the way he said it, Emily couldn't be sure whether Philip meant "a time like Christmas" or "at a time I feel defeated." But it didn't matter because the kids encircled him, the girls showed him their goodies from their grandparents, and Greg couldn't stop talking about his license plate.

"No reason to stop now, is there?" Philip asked.

The children shouted, "Emily! Emily! Where are the presents for Emily?" as packages began to come toward her from every direction.

Clint and Greg had gone together and gotten her a set of writing pens with tiny roses engraved on them. "They're for your books," Clint said as she turned them over and examined them. "Bethany keeps reminding us that you're going to be a famous author someday soon."

"Thank you, both," she said with pleasure.

She opened a robe with matching slippers and a bottle of expensive perfume from her father, a crème-colored sweater from Bethany and Lisa—which resulted in hugs all around—and a blue crocheted afghan from Amanda's parents.

"Here's another," Philip said as he pressed a small package in her hands.

"What's this?" she asked.

"Something from me," he answered.

Emily tore open the paper and lifted the lid on the interesting round box. "Careful," he warned her once, and then he said nothing more. When Emily pulled the tiny crystal bird out of its holder and held it high, even the tiny upturned tail feathers glowed in a hundred separate hues as it reflected the glow from the Christmas tree.

"It's beautiful," she said, scarcely able to speak. "Philip, it's..." She didn't want to say anything more, not here, not in front of the whole family. He'd made her happy enough just by arriving, and now this. Shyly she handed him a small box, too, a money clip and a business-card case engraved with his initials. He cradled them both in his hand for a long time, just looking at her.

"You didn't have to," he said.

"Neither did you," she said.

They sat, looking at each other, smiling.

Emily didn't recognize the return address when Bethany handed her the next parcel. It took Emily a beat, two beats, to recognize the spidery handwriting. The tilt of the letters brought back a rush of memories for Emily, some happy, some sad, all poignant. She hadn't expected to hear from her mother this Christmas.

"Who's that one from?" Bethany asked, scooting closer.

"My mother." She struggled for words. She glanced across at Philip. "A real surprise." Of all the people in the room, Philip could understand how much a gift from her mother would mean.

Inside, she found a green leather-bound book with blank pages. A journal for her thoughts and maybe even her Baby Sprout stories. She leafed through it, then laid the journal on her lap. With one clenched fist, Emily clung to the arm of the chair, like she might be holding on to a world where everything had its place, the world where she found peace, here at the farm.

One by one that night, the family settled around the table in the brightly lit kitchen for a steaming cup of hot chocolate. One by one, they tired and went to bed. Amanda's parents wandered away, yawning. Lisa and Bethany hugged Emily good-night. Clint stayed at the table to visit with his brother and then he disappeared, too. Emily, Philip and Greg found him later sitting in the family room staring at the presents still waiting beneath the tree. There was still a pile of them, wrapped in brightly colored paper, and no one knew when they would be opened. Gifts for Amanda.

"Dad." Greg wrapped his arms around his father's chest. "Why don't you take them to her?" The boy paused hopefully. "I could go with you."

"No, son." Then, "But would you all mind if I went to the hospital, though? It's Christmas Eve. I'd like to sit with her a while."

Emily admired how well Clint had done today, hiding the loneliness he felt because his wife wasn't here to share the holiday. He'd done a good job with his sadness, trying to keep things jovial for his children.

With her hand on Philip's arm, she waited to hear what Greg would say.

Clint continued, "I just…well, it's Christmas Eve."

Greg didn't hesitate. "Go ahead. Go stay the night. We'll be okay."

"But if you should need me for anything…"

"We're all here together," Greg said. Philip and Emily nodded. "Granddad's here, too. I can take care of anything that comes up."

Clint picked up one of the presents. He hugged it to him as if just touching her gift would bring Amanda closer to him, closer to waking, closer to living. "Okay." He rumpled his son's hair in gratitude. "I'll go, then."

Only Philip and Emily remained in the kitchen after Clint drove away. Greg headed out to the garage, and Philip was quiet for a moment before he spoke.

"That gift. From your mother. You weren't expecting it, were you?"

"No."

He watched her stirring her chocolate, chasing a marshmallow with her spoon. "Quite a Christmas, isn't it?"

Emily didn't know what to say about her mother's gift. She'd gotten so used to hoping. So used to expecting her mother to change and winding up disappointed. It had been so many years. Did she dare hope that things would change now?

"If you'd only been there the Christmases she forgot, the time Daddy had to hurry around town at four o'clock on Christmas Eve to find something, anything, so I'd have a gift from her underneath the tree. And then came the holidays when my father had to drive around looking for her. He'd leave me by myself until he could find her and bring her home."

"She didn't forget you this year," Philip reminded her gently.

Emily picked up the new journal and fingered it. There were years of her childhood that still needed to be accounted for.

"I know. I was at church tonight, and I was thinking—"

Philip's mug stopped halfway to his lips. "You went to church?"

Her eyes shot to his and she remembered what she'd told him. She remembered how she'd told him she'd never trust God again. But her heart had begun to melt tonight, because of Bethany's prayer, because of a quiet reassurance that spoke in her heart.

"I did. Clint invited me." Then, "I didn't realize how badly I needed it."

Philip placed the mug in the exact center of his napkin.

"I was thinking how hard it is to hold on to so much anger."

Emily couldn't help it. Christmas had always been a time that brought out the most difficult memories. She remembered every detail as clearly as if it had been yesterday, the night she'd gone caroling when she'd been close to Lisa's age, how, one by one, they'd stopped at each of their own homes to sing for their own parents. At every house they'd been greeted by hot chocolate and warm squeezes, cheerful applause and well-wishing—the love other families shared, the vacancy that her father always tried to make amends for. She didn't dare let anyone see her haggard father, her mother who was probably so drunk that she would go reeling off the front porch as they sang to her.

She didn't want any of her friends to see that the dishes hadn't been washed for three days and the walls that were filled with holes from where her mother had kicked through the plaster. So, "This is my house," she'd said to her friends, pointing out another place in the neighborhood with a wreath on the door and a view of a cozy room inside. "No reason to stop, though. There isn't anybody home."

After the party, when a mother had offered to drive her back home, she had gotten out of the car and walked proudly to the strange porch while her stomach churned. She waited until the carload of girls drove away before she bundled up against the cold and walked to her real home, which had been a good mile away. And no one at school had ever known the difference, thank goodness.

How can I let something like that go?

"The gift she sent. Maybe she wants to come back into your life, Emily."

But Emily shook her head. "It's going to take a lot more than just one leather-bound book to prove that to me. There are years of my childhood that need to be accounted for."

"You talk about how much it drains you to hold on to the anger. Maybe the way to let it go is to be able to forgive her," he said.

She asked, "And what about you, Philip? You speak of me forgiving someone. What about you?"

"What do you mean?" he asked her.

"There's one person you're even angrier at than Morgan Brockner," Emily said. "Philip, what about forgiving yourself?"

He stared at her. He carried his mug to the sink and ran water into it. "We each make our own choices, don't we? It seems so simple when we each try to speak for the other."

"Yes."

It seemed he didn't want to talk anymore. Philip's expression had hardened. Emily knew she had said too much. He didn't look at her again as she headed outside to go to sleep in her own cabin.

Chapter Ten

As Emily lay in the cabin, still wide awake, she heard a cow bawling in the distance. Something sounded different about the cows tonight. Their lowing was usually such a warm, reassuring, peaceful murmur. Tonight it sounded frantic. Emily wondered if something could be wrong with one of the cows. Surely Clint would take care of it. Then she remembered that Clint was spending the night at the hospital with Amanda.

Emily lay there, tense, listening, and then she heard footsteps in the grass outside the cabin. She was up and throwing on her flannel robe before she heard the pounding on the cabin door. She flung open the door and found Greg standing there. He must have been running. He gasped for breath.

"What's wrong?"

"It's Honey Snookems." He was breathing so hard that he could barely talk. "I need you to help me." Emily ran into the bathroom and threw on a shirt and some jeans while Greg talked. "I was out walking. I was thinking about Dad and worried about Mom and I heard Honey Snookems bawling. She's in this old corral, the one close to the cabin. I guess she felt safe there."

"Is she calving?"

"She's doing her best. I think the calf's stuck. We've got to help her or we're going to lose both of them. Uncle Philip was at the corral when I found her."

"Oh, Greg."

"We've got to throw her, get her to lie down, or there's no way we can get to the calf and help her. Uncle Philip sent me to find you. Dad's still at the hospital."

"Can your grandfather help us?"

"There isn't time to go back to the main house and get him. We've got to throw her now."

Emily was out the door then, running toward the rickety fenced corral and stable, with Greg following right behind her. When they got to the stable, Philip was there trying to stroke Honey Snookems and calm her. "Oh, Emily," he said. "Thank goodness you're here."

Honey Snookems was hunched up and frightened in the corner of the corral, and she wouldn't let any of them approach her. "I should have known something like this was about to happen." Greg spoke softly so he wouldn't spook her. "She was skittish all evening. I should have said something to Dad but I just wasn't thinking about cows tonight. It's too late now to even call the vet. He won't get here in time."

"Poor little mama," Emily crooned as she moved toward the animal that she had learned to love. "Poor little mama." Her voice was steady, but it did nothing to quiet the cow. Instead, the animal moved farther away from them and hunched in another corner. "Oh, Philip—" Emily spun to face him "—tell us what to do. This is horrible. We've got to help her."

"I've delivered a calf or two with Clint." Philip's voice turned quiet. His confidence calmed her. He gestured toward his nephew. "This is the guy who will tell us what needs to be done." He knew his brother had taught Greg well.

Greg took command of the situation. "Keep talking to her," he advised Emily. "She needs reassurance. She won't want anything to do with people right now, but having someone she knows just talk to her may help her relax."

"Okay." Emily did as she was told.

"We've got to get her to lie down. I can't do

anything for her with her standing like this. I don't know how much more she can handle."

"We can't lose this cow, Greg," Emily almost whispered as she shook her head vehemently. "This family can't handle losing anything else."

Greg didn't hear her comment. He was already in the tack room of the old stable searching for supplies.

"We can do it, Emily." Philip had heard what she said. "We have to." Without thinking, he gripped her by the shoulders and began to slowly knead her muscles with strong fingers. "You okay?"

"I'm fine." She leaned back against him and closed her eyes as the fear and the frustration she felt seemed to ebb away. "Come on, mama cow." She spoke to Honey again while she drew on Philip's strength. This time, Honey Snookems moved as if she was responding to Emily's voice. The animal moved toward Emily as if she had found a kindred spirit. Her forelegs began to bend beneath her.

"She's going down on her own." Philip scarcely dared to breathe for fear of frightening the animal into standing up again. But by the time Greg arrived back at the corral carrying chains, hooks and a rope, the cow was kneeling on all fours in the corner by the stable.

"Amen." Greg's sigh of thanks was full of relief. "She's down." Despite his worry, he turned and winked at Emily. "I guess you can go back to bed now. Uncle Philip and I don't need you anymore. That's why I came to get you, so you could pick her up and lay her on her side for me."

"Give me a break." Emily wagged a finger at him as she stroked Honey's fuzzy head with her other hand. "This cow probably weighs six hundred pounds. And that's when she's not expecting a calf."

"Pretty close," Greg admitted as he laughed and Emily laughed, too. Their laughter was a welcome relief, taking the edge off their tension. "I didn't particularly want to throw her myself, either."

Honey Snookems was mooing for all she was worth now, and Emily felt certain the pathetic sound would wake the girls and Amanda's parents back at the main house. "Sit up by her head and keep talking to her the way you've been doing." It was strange how calm Greg seemed, Philip thought, as he obeyed his nephew's instructions. Once again, he thought how much he admired the boy. He thought how strong Greg was, how much he could help his father if Clint would only let him. And Emily was thinking the same thing. Greg did dumb things occasionally to prove he was becoming an adult, but under pressure, he remained levelheaded and mature. He embodied the best of both his father and his uncle, Emily reflected.

"I've got to get up the birth canal some way and figure out which way the calf is lying. We'll wrap the chains around the calf's front legs and do our best to pull it. That's when I'm really going to need both of you." He glanced up at his uncle and Emily.

Greg worked gently with Honey Snookems and cooed to her. Finally, after what seemed like an eternity, he looked up and Emily sensed his discouragement. "Why does Dad have to be gone tonight? I'm the one who told him to go. I can't reach the calf. I can't get my arms far enough."

"Let me try." Emily rose to her feet, careful not to alarm Honey. "My arms may be longer than yours, more slender."

"You'd be willing to try?" There was a touch of hope in Greg's voice now. Philip stooped down beside them as Greg gently guided Emily's arms where they needed to go.

"It's okay, Honey. It's okay," she crooned. And as she stretched her arms to try to reach the baby, Philip got the feeling that everything in his life until now had been a fantasy, a mere shadow of the truth. He'd been a grown-up little boy playing grown-up games, and look what he'd been missing. All of it, his reputation, his business, his past, was diminished by comparison to this one moment, watching Emily fighting to save a new little life. *Father, I let Morgan Brockner steal everything from me, and it had nothing to do with my company.* He had been crazy to forget about his family here on the farm during the past two months. He had been desolate at the thought of losing his business. But he stood the chance of losing all this, too.

Emily glanced across at Greg as he knelt beside her, and she realized that she was acting calm and deliberate because Philip sat at her side. She wanted to prove something to him. As if somehow saving this calf would take some of her disappointment about life away, too. Being around Philip made Emily want to be deserving of him. It made Emily want to overcome the anger and the unforgiveness that had been controlling her for so long. "There." Her voice was triumphant. She could feel the calf.

"Take this chain and hook it around the calf's forehocks," Greg instructed her. "It's a little confusing. I've done this once before and I'm almost certain the head is up this direction. I can tell by the shape." He pushed his hand against Honey's hind section.

"Okay." Emily took a deep breath. She grasped the chains he handed her along with some rope and carefully worked the rope up inside Honey's belly. She could feel something there, some hint of life, the spindly legs, the wet fur. She thought at first she couldn't detect movement. But then she felt a slight flinch. Emily didn't know if the calf should be moving at this point. She would be glad when this part of the delivery was over. Her arms ached.

"You're doing fine." Philip stooped behind her now, pushing against her shoulders. His firm pressure gave her the extra endurance she needed.

"There. I've got it," she told them both. "I can't tell exactly where it is, but I know I've got it."

Greg said from behind them, "We've got to get that calf out quickly." He picked the ends of the chains up out of the dust and began to tug out the slack. Then he pulled harder, but nothing happened. Once more Greg strained against the chains and then, slowly, the tiny forehocks began to slide out of the birth canal. Greg motioned once more to Philip and Emily. "I need you both. Emily, can you reach up again and direct the calf's head? Uncle Philip, I need you to help me pull."

Emily obeyed him without question. Without realizing what she was doing, as she positioned herself, she was talking to the calf, begging it to be okay, begging it to be born so its mother would live, too. "Come on," she said over and over again. "Come on, little one. We're not going to lose you."

Philip locked his arms around his nephew's waist and eased back until Greg's weight was centered against him. Then together they pulled.

The calf's head was born easily but, after that, their progress came to a grinding halt. "I was afraid of this," Greg groaned. "Her hips are stuck. Hip-locked, it's called. And there's nothing else we can do except what we've been doing."

Emily repositioned herself between Greg and Philip. She locked her arms around Greg's shoulders and Philip locked his arms around her waist, and for long, excruciating minutes they yanked as hard as they could, but nothing happened. Honey Snookems had gone quiet. She was exhausted, on the verge of giving up, and Emily wanted to scream. It all seemed so hopeless. She turned to Philip and he glimpsed the resignation in her eyes. "I can't stand much more of this."

Just as she spoke, Honey Snookems started to bawl again. "Come on," Philip urged. "One more time." They tugged. Tugged again, and this time, with their second effort, the hind legs slid out with a great sucking sound and the calf was born.

Honey Snookems nosed the tiny form and

mooed at it. But the calf did not respond. Instead, the tiny body remained still.

"We didn't make it." Emily just stood there staring at the unmoving tiny carcass on the ground. She felt so numb with disbelief that she couldn't cry.

Greg didn't make a sound. Instead, his legs buckled beneath him, and he collapsed beside the calf. Emily couldn't feel anything except Philip's arms still locked desperately around her waist. She turned to face him, and he took her head in his hand and guided it gently to his shoulder and there it remained. Philip wanted to comfort both Emily and Greg but there was nothing he could say. He did the only thing he could do—he brushed his lips in a light desperate kiss atop Emily's head. As if that gesture alone gave her the strength to do what she knew she must do, she glanced up at Philip, touched his jaw then and with tears in her eyes turned to Greg. She only knew that she had to comfort this young man who had experienced yet another loss. "Greg," she said softly as she moved toward him and gripped his arm. "Greg. I'm sorry."

Streaks of dust and tears and sweat ran down the teen's face as he shook his head at her. "I should have known it would end this way. If Dad had been here, we wouldn't have lost this calf." He managed a brave, halfhearted smile. "We gave it a fierce try, though, didn't we?"

"Yeah," Philip said from behind her. "We did." Emily turned toward Philip again, and she glimpsed a familiar melancholy expression in his eyes. She realized then that his arms were still around her. It was as if he needed something to hold on to just as desperately as she did, and Emily stood next to him, thanking him with her eyes for being there. It had been a long night for all of them.

Finally Philip pulled his gaze away from Emily's. "Where can I find a shovel?" he asked his nephew. "I want to bury this calf before the sun comes up. This is going to be hard enough as it is. Lisa and Bethany have been so excited about Honey Snookems's calf." He caressed Honey's nose when he passed her, going to look for the implement he needed. "I'm glad we saved this mama cow." He looked sad as he spoke. "We could have easily lost them both, you know."

"You dumb old cow," Greg bellowed at Honey Snookems just a little too loudly. "You always were the one to get yourself into messes." Tears coursed down the boy's cheeks.

Philip came back with a shovel and propped it up against the corral fence before he went to his nephew and wrapped his arms around Greg's shoulders. "Birthing that cow was a brave thing, Greg. No matter what the outcome, I'm proud of you. I know your father will be, too."

Greg spun around to face his uncle. "He won't be proud. He doesn't trust me. He doesn't think I'm mature enough to handle any responsibility. He'll think I screwed this up. He'll think it's my fault that Honey's calf died."

"But Honey didn't die, Greg." Emily moved up beside them and gripped Greg's arm. As the boy spoke, she had begun to realize that the boy's distress went much deeper than just bereavement over a calf that hadn't survived. The pain went clear down to Greg's soul. His father was keeping him from his mother's bedside out of a sense of love, no matter how misdirected that move might be. And Greg didn't interpret it that way. "You're laying the blame on yourself. For the calf. For your mother. For the pressure your father is under."

Greg looked up at her.

Philip could tell by Greg's face that she was interpreting Greg's thoughts correctly. Of course she was. It was easy for her. The subjects she was discussing were dear to her heart. She could just as easily have been talking about herself.

"Don't blame yourself for something that

you're not responsible for," Emily continued. "Personally, I think you should be allowed to visit Amanda at the hospital. I'd be willing to go with you and talk to your father about it, if you want me to. But no matter what he says to you or whether he lets you go see her, just remember how capable you are." The words in her head seemed to come from somewhere outside herself. "Just remember what a great young man you're growing into."

When Philip walked away from them, he turned toward Honey. She had moved away from the calf and she was not bawling, but she was hunched up again just the way she had been when they had first found her. "Emily!" he cried out. "Greg! Get over here. This crazy cow is having another calf."

Greg was beside the animal immediately with Emily right behind him, and this time, Honey Snookems had a much easier time of it. Philip stood with his arms around Emily's shoulders, bracing her against him in the early-morning moonlight. Greg delivered the second calf himself. "Dumb cow," he crooned over and over again as he guided the calf's head down the birth canal with his hands. "Crazy, dumb cow. Twins. I can't believe this."

When the second calf was born, Honey nosed it and licked it off and it moved immediately. The little guy was all wet fur and gangly legs. The tears streamed down Greg's face. Emily laughed and Philip applauded when Honey Snookems stood and then nosed persistently until the tiny calf stood, too, and nursed.

It was three in the morning by the time Philip walked Emily back to the camp house. The stars shone like pinpoints as the two of them walked along toward Emily's adopted home. Christmas morning, and all was right with the world. They had shared so much during the past hours that it seemed good and true and right to be together, walking homeward through the night, absorbing the silence.

"Hey!" Philip broke the spell first as he pointed to a flashing red light crossing the sky. It could have been anything, a meteor or a star or an airplane. "I'll bet that's Santa Claus. I'll bet his night has been almost as long as ours has."

"Yeah." Emily peered into the sky in the direction he was pointing. "I wonder if he's stopped at our house yet. With all the excitement Honey put us through, I forgot that Santa was supposed to show up tonight." She grinned up at him and then her smile turned to concern. "You still look exhausted, Philip." She could see the lines under his eyes even in the moonlight. "This restful holiday with the family hasn't done you much good."

He chuckled and it was a warm sound, a sound that seemed to ripple out into the night and bind the two of them closer together. "Oh, yes it has."

Emily spoke again. "I'm going to call Mother tomorrow." She hesitated when she realized how late it was. "Today…a little later, after the sun comes up. I think I can get her number from Information. I have the return address on the package she sent."

"What are you going to tell her?" They were outside the cabin now, and Philip turned and studied her expression.

"Whatever comes to mind, I guess. Thanks for the Christmas gift. Thanks for remembering me. Stuff like that." Almost anything was going to be very hard for her to say.

"I think you'll be glad you did it."

Silence. Emily said nothing for a long time.

"Are you tired?" he asked. A ridiculous question. But for a moment he didn't know what else to talk about.

"Tired but not sleepy," she answered honestly. "I can't wait until the sun comes up on that new little calf. I want to get a closer look at him. And Bethany and Lisa are going to think that little guy is their best Christmas present ever."

"You're right." As Philip looked down at her, there was something in her face, that same openness she always showed him, coupled with the fatigue from the past few hours, that made him realize what he was missing out on. She was beautiful and fragile and so different from Morgan. She wasn't just a feisty ad copywriter or a confused, sad woman who was taking care of the kids to prove something to herself. She was Emily. He realized suddenly how much he cared for her and respected her. She had done quite a job helping to deliver that calf tonight.

"Philip?" Her eyes were filled with questions as she reached up and gingerly touched his cheek. "What are you thinking?"

When he didn't answer, she sensed that he was troubled. One minute he was her confidant and the next he was somebody else—a professional totally wrapped up in his career and his company, someone who stayed distant and determined. She wasn't always certain what to expect from him.

She turned away from him and gazed up at the stars. "When the second calf was born, I was thinking what a wonderful sign of renewal it was. To Greg. To me." She faced him again. "So much happened at church tonight, it's made me start feeling like I'm the one who needs to be forgiven for something. I'll always wonder why Mother didn't love me as much as she loved her drinking. But maybe I'm wrong to resent her for it. Maybe it's time I began to forgive her."

"What do you mean?" Philip asked cautiously. "What do you mean, 'So much happened at church tonight'?"

He could see the haunting doubt on her face when she turned toward him. "I think I was wrong to let go of my faith so easily. All this time, instead of letting it go, I think I was supposed to let it take me somewhere."

A consuming tenderness welled up in Philip. As he looked at her, he remembered a hundred other times in his life when he had been watching an associate or a friend have to learn something without his assistance. Watching Emily learning to trust Jesus again was like watching a child learning to walk. He wanted to reach out and grasp her each time he saw her lose her confidence. But he couldn't do that for her, not when he cared this much about her. He had to let her take each step on her own.

"Bethany prayed for you during the candlelight service," Emily said. "She prayed that you wouldn't be alone last night."

"Well, see," he answered. "Think back to the things you told Greg tonight in the corral," Philip reminded her. "You told him to stop blaming himself for something that had never been his fault. You told him to recognize his own capabilities as a person."

There was something in her eyes then, some small spark that Philip guessed might be hope. "Those are the same things I should have been saying to myself all along, aren't they?" she asked.

"I think they are," he replied.

Emily turned away from him and gazed up into the night sky. There were a billion stars blazing overhead and, at that moment, she felt that each one of them was shining for her. When she finally spoke, her voice sounded very small. "I sent my Baby Sprout manuscript to a children's publisher last week." Philip was the first person she had told. It still scared her, thinking that her manuscript might be sitting on a desk somewhere, waiting for acceptance. She grinned up at him. It made her feel better about it, knowing that they were in this together. "I sent your storyboards in, too."

Philip's eyes widened. He knew what submitting the manuscript meant to her. He picked her up and spun her around; then he set her back on the ground in front of him. "What a Christmas Eve this has been," he almost shouted.

Emily grinned. "It's Christmas morning now." The sky was just beginning to glow a faint apricot against the eastern horizon. It was almost sunup. "Come on in the cabin and I'll fix you a cup of coffee, Mr. Manning." She pulled the screen door open and he followed her inside.

He sat down at the little kitchen table and watched her while she rummaged through the cabinets to find things she needed—the battered aluminum coffeepot, a spoon, the matches, a can of coffee—and that's how they started their new day.

As the two of them walked hand in hand toward the main house and as they neared the corral by the house, Emily recognized the familiar bawling coming from the stable. But this time she heard laughter there, too. Bethany and Lisa had already discovered Honey Snookems's new calf.

"What's going on in here?" Philip called as they neared the barn.

"Come look at what we found," Lisa urged them.

"We named her something really special," Bethany chimed in. "We're going to call her Baby Sprout."

Philip scooped his youngest niece up in his arms. "Where did you two come up with such a poetic name?" he asked. "And so original, too." He winked at Emily.

"I think it's perfect," Emily said, grinning from ear to ear. Bethany and Lisa giggled when Philip stuck his tongue out at her.

Emily couldn't resist giggling, too, as all of them headed back toward the house.

Amanda's mother was in the kitchen when Emily arrived. The house smelled of cinnamon rolls. Emily sliced the venison sausage, a treat Clint provided every Christmas morning from his hunting trips, and the girls helped her in the kitchen. The aroma of the meat wafted through as the sausage sizzled on the stove.

As the venison cooked, Emily found the chance to slip away and join Philip on the porch.

He was already bent over a canvas with newspapers and paints spread out all around him. He was so engrossed in his work that he didn't hear her approaching. Gazing into the distance, Philip was trying to re-create with his brush the colors he'd seen in the morning sky.

"Hi." Emily spoke softly so she wouldn't startle him.

He turned to her with one arm and looped it around her legs in a motion for her to sit beside him.

"I can't stay," she explained, touching his shoulder gently. "I have to put the eggs on."

He turned from his work and grinned up at her,

a haphazard, cocky sort of smile that made him look like a little boy instead of a man in his thirties. "You're wonderful, you know," he told her.

"So are you." She gazed lovingly at him for a moment, at his nose, at his lips, at the faraway expression in his eyes as he gazed over the horizon. "What are you painting?"

He held the rough sketch up so she could see it. She could make out the pencil outline of a mother cow nursing her newborn calf. He had already painted in the soft colors of the sunrise.

"Oh, Philip," she whispered.

"Breakfast is ready!" Lisa called out.

"Oops." Emily grinned at Philip sheepishly. "Sounds like somebody else got stuck doing the eggs."

"That's okay," Philip whispered. "I'd rather you stayed here with me."

The entire family assembled around the dining room table while Lisa poured coffee. And even Greg was grinning when he came downstairs.

Clint reached out to his son and hugged him. "I'm proud of you, son," he said, his eyes shining.

"Thanks, Dad."

Clint had arrived home shortly after sunup. He had slept in Amanda's room at the hospital almost all night. And there was something about him this

Christmas morning—an extra sense of hopefulness that made him seem more like his former self to his family.

"How is she, Dad?" Lisa was the first one brave enough to ask, and Clint surprised everyone when he glanced up from his plate.

"She's doing much better, Lisa."

Amanda's parents both stared at their son-in-law. Clint saw their expressions and answered their unasked questions. "She's gaining weight. She gained twelve ounces in the past week." Amanda survived on the intravenous glucose and proteins the doctors poured into her body. The fact that her body was finally accepting that nourishment was a major victory.

But that was only the beginning of Clint's story. Late last night, he had spent his time with her reading her their Christmas cards. He had brought the entire stack from the top of the spinet piano in the family room, and he had gone through them all, talking about the verses and describing the photographs and naming old friends. There were oodles of kids all over the country that Clint had never met, with names like Samantha and Eric and Lisa Jo, who meant something to them because he and Amanda had once been friends with their parents. He read to her about their accomplishments, their band trips and their National Merit Scholarships. He spoke to her about their own kids, Bethany and Lisa and Greg, and he listed the things they had accomplished and talked to her about the things that made him proud of them.

He'd been talking about all three children—first, about Greg driving the Studebaker and studying for exams and next about how Bethany teased her brother sometimes—when he'd looked up and, centimeter by centimeter, in an obviously deliberate movement, Manderly had placed her hand on his. Actually, it had been an almost imperceptible movement, one that could easily have been explained away by a reflex, but Clint had too much faith. He knew it was something more than that, her not waking up but touching him, and this time even the doctors had been impressed. She'd been kept under close observation throughout the night but no more movement had been noted. Finally, Clint had fallen asleep on a cot beside her, and carolers had sung outside in the hallway while Manderly had lain sleeping silently, her breathing strong and steady.

Of course, later in Clint's study, the two brothers couldn't get through their time together without discussing the court case today. Never mind that it was Christmas.

"Bennett Huff has been working around the clock, trying to fight off this litigation," Philip told his brother. "You know the stories have been all over the media in Dallas. I'm hoping most of our clients will stick with us, but I don't know. This shouldn't have to be your problem, Clint. It's Manning Real Estate and Investment that she wants." *And my head on a silver platter.* "I'm sorry. I hate it that your name's involved, too."

"What if it is?" Clint clapped his brother on the back. "If I lose clients over this, then I'll know they're clients I didn't want to represent in the first place." Where Philip's faith still foundered, Clint's had been bolstered by Amanda's hand making a slight movement toward his last night, her fingers draping over his own.

"You've stood beside me during plenty of battles," Clint reminded him. "Now it's my turn to stand with you, side by side."

"I don't want this to hurt your business—"

"We'll fight Morgan Brockner with everything we've got."

Philip raked his fingers through his hair. "You have no idea how much it means to me to hear you say that, brother."

"Oh, you're wrong about that," Clint reminded him. "I have an idea. I know exactly how much it means. Because you are the one who has always been standing by me."

Emily dialed and gave the telephone operator the information she needed to track her mother's phone number. She held her breath, uncertain how to feel, waiting for the voice to confirm the address and the name. "Here's the number you requested," the operator told her before a computer voice came on the line to give out the area code and digits.

Father, she prayed. *If this is what You want me to do, then give me the words. I can't do it without You.*

Philip paused beside her, gripped her arm. "You want me to stay in the room while you talk to her?"

Emily nodded. She'd never been so grateful. Philip gave her so much strength, just standing beside her. Then she heard the voice answer on the other end of the line.

"Hello?"

"Mother?"

"Emily? Is that you?" As always, her voice sounded so shrill and sharp that Emily held the phone away from her ear. *"Is that you?"*

"Yes. It's me."

The woman didn't hesitate before she began to

interrogate her. "What's wrong? Why are you calling? What's happened?"

"No, Mother. Nothing's wrong. I just… wanted to call."

"Oh."

"I got the gift you sent. We opened presents last night here on the farm. I just wanted you to know how happy I was—" Emily paused, searching for the right words "—that you thought of me."

"Oh, well." The woman's voice tinged with sarcasm. "You're my daughter, aren't you?"

"Yes, but—" *But you've never done anything like this before.*

"But, what?"

Emily took a deep breath and finished the sentence. "How did you know that a journal would be the perfect thing to send?"

"Since you gave up your *professional* position," her mother said, "I started wondering what you were doing with all the extra time you have on your hands."

Here it comes. Emily caught herself bristling. *Even when I call to thank her for a gift, she's going to make sure I know she disapproves of me.*

Words resounded in her head again, as clearly as if someone had walked up to her and started speaking. She glanced at Philip. She took so much comfort in the way he clenched her shoulder, supporting her.

These were the words that came into Emily's head. *Beloved, to the hungry even the bitter tastes sweet.*

"Mother..."

"I keep remembering how it was when you were a little girl. All those hours you would sit at the table with paper, writing stories. I never encouraged you much, and you were so cute, you were always concentrating so hard!"

"You...you watched me when I was writing stories?"

"Oh, all the time. There was one about an elephant trapped in a village in India, do you remember that one? He couldn't get home because, every time he turned around, he ran into something with his trunk."

Emily hadn't thought of that old story for years.

"I helped you research that. We went to the library and read *National Geographic*. To find the right village in India. To learn about elephants."

Emily was stunned. "I *do* remember that story." Then, "I didn't remember you took me to the library. I thought it was Daddy."

Her mother let that comment slip by. "I've been thinking of you, Em, finally having a little time to yourself in the country, changing your life around a bit. I've been thinking maybe you would find time to write for yourself there."

"I—" Emily wondered if she should say something about her manuscript. Maybe her mother would use the book as something else to deride her about. But something nudged her to share this, to let her mother know how timely the journal had been. "You may think I'm crazy, but I submitted a story to a publisher this month." Then, "I'll let you know if I hear anything about it."

"I think that's *wonderful.* So good to see you pursuing the desires of your heart. They've been put there for a reason, you know."

Emily didn't know what to say. How would her mother know anything about the desires of her heart? She held on to the receiver with both hands as if she could hang on to the years they'd lost together. Her mind whirred. Blood pounded in her ears. Then she pulled herself together.

They discussed many topics. She talked about Clint's children. Her mother mentioned that she'd joined a bridge club. *Mother,* she wanted to ask when the conversation came to a lull and she knew it was time for her to hang up. *Why now? Why couldn't you have been there for me years ago?* There was a pause. "Mother..." Emily hated the quaver she heard in her voice. "It was good talking to you."

When Emily turned to Philip after she'd hung up the phone, she couldn't stop shaking. She tried to smile, but that didn't hide the tears in her eyes.

"Emily," he whispered as he bundled her against him, holding her tight in his arms.

"I don't know what I'm going to do," she said, her voice thick.

"You're going to take it a day at a time."

At this moment Emily knew she owed her spirit and her courage and her self-esteem to the God who had brought this new family into her life. And the only thing she could think of was that she might be falling in love with Philip as he gently rocked her back and forth while she cried.

Chapter Eleven

Philip stared at the papers he held. Here it was, with his name printed in bold type at the top of the page. It was real. This trial was going to happen.

> Morgan Brockner/Brockner Associates, Plaintiff, *vs.* Philip Bradley Manning/Manning Commercial Real Estate and Investment, Inc., Defendant, for contract infringement, compensatory damages in the amount of $3.7 million and personal damages for undue suffering and loss of reputation in the amount of $7 million more.

If the judgment went in her favor, Philip would have to scrape the bottom of the barrel to pay off the settlement. But he wasn't planning on losing to her, and if he did, the important part of his company, the building, the associates, the clients, would remain intact. It was his reputation he stood to lose. But he didn't plan on putting that in jeopardy, either.

He was glad the pretrial consultation was over. He had been dreading it since before Christmas. And now he had another month's reprieve until the trial began. The trial had been moved up several weeks, and Philip didn't know whether it was by luck or by design. He was ready to get the farce over with. He speculated that Morgan was, too.

His brother's words echoed in his head. "We'll fight her with everything we've got." Philip hadn't had any idea how much it would encourage him to have his brother standing by his side.

The pretrial conference had been simple. Bennett Huff had done his best to talk him into settling out of court. But Philip wouldn't hear of it. It might save him time that way and it might save him money in the long run, but he refused to take the easy way out with Morgan. He wanted to fight her, and if all of America wanted to stand at the bull pen and watch, then that was okay with him, too.

Besides, it seemed to Philip that settling out

of court might just as well be an admission of guilt. Huff thought that if the board of directors would agree to it, settling out of court would keep the drama of the trial out of the newspapers. But Philip knew better. They weren't dealing with a predictable opponent here. They were dealing with Morgan Brockner. Philip was certain that if he settled out of court, Morgan would find a way to get news of the settlement into the headlines, too.

And so they had gone about the business of finalizing the specifics of the trial before they "went at it," as Bennett Huff had once phrased it. They sat at separate tables with an army of attorneys and met with District Judge Keslow Wilson to work out the details.

Philip wasn't surprised at all when Morgan requested a jury trial. In a civil matter like this one, despite the phenomenal amount of money involved, the case could have been tried by the judge. It would have saved them at least a week of jury selection at the onset of the trial. But Morgan wouldn't hear of it. She had to have a jury, and Philip suspected it was because she wanted as many people involved in this trial as possible. The average layman was much more interested in what a jury decided than what a judge set forth.

And because Morgan requested it, even though he didn't want it, the Brockner *vs.* Manning trial would be a trial by jury. Philip had thrown his hands up at her when he'd left the room. *Let her do what she wants to do,* he'd thought. *Hopefully, she'll find out in the end that it's all been a waste of time.* "Lord," he prayed. "You are the only one who can see an end to this."

When he went back to his office, Philip was exhausted. He and Bennett Huff had been going over papers and talking to witnesses and analyzing all the facts until Philip felt that every time he sat down in his chair he was making a calculated movement. He stared at the watercolor on the wall and thought of the farm and of how far away he felt from all the people there. He had only been able to make it to the farm twice since Christmas because of this trial—once on New Year's Day for a family celebration and once at the end of February to celebrate Bethany's birthday.

And it had been a wonderful party for his niece. Emily had planned it, and there had been kids and balloons and pizzas all over the place. Eight girls from Bethany's fourth-grade class had slept over on a Friday night, and Philip had found it hard, with all the ruckus going on, to talk to anybody. And so he had watched Emily all evening long as she prepared her fifth pepperoni-and-mushroom pizza and poured what was perhaps the fiftieth paper cup full of orange soda.

Philip had seen how tired she'd been and then he had remembered some of the parties his mom had hostessed for him, and he'd realized that giving a birthday party for a child took a lot of love and a great amount of patience. And then he'd remembered Emily's telling him once that she had never been brave enough to invite any of her friends to her house to spend the night. He wondered if Emily's mother had ever given any birthday parties for her. Emily was giving the girl one of the things she'd always wanted and had never had, a slumber party. With bubbly, giggly girls who played records and whispered secrets about boys and ate all night long.

Philip had always loved visiting the farm, but now that he knew Emily was there, he liked it even more. The house seemed alive again, the way it had been before Amanda's illness. The girls laughed freely again and his brother seemed less subdued, more prone to giving his opinion and, like his daughters, to laughing. Even Greg seemed content. Emily Lattrell had worked miracles with his family.

And it was fun now just to call the farm, just hoping she would answer, so he could hear her voice.

Philip was certain that the legal battle between the two companies would be emphasized in the local media. He knew how Morgan worked. He expected certain details of their romantic relationship to be splashed across the front pages of Texas newspapers and the *Wall Street Journal,* as well. Emily had asked pointed questions about Morgan before. Certainly, this trial would bring to light every detail about his former relationship with the woman.

One thing Philip was certain of: he did not want to underestimate the impact this trial would have on Emily. She had been so fragile and forlorn when she had come to the farm.

Philip knew he was watching Emily learn how to trust, and he didn't want anything he and Morgan had done to stand in the way of that.

Philip told her the rest of the story then, not with all the details, but he included the things he thought she should know. He told her he had cared for Morgan in college and about the way she had betrayed him.

In fact, knowing those things about Philip did make Emily feel different about him. She was comparing herself to him, knowing that he had lost an important part of himself, too, when Morgan had left him and his company to start building her own.

The jury selection in the Brockner *vs.* Manning trial took exactly one week. The jurors streamed through the room and Bennett Huff questioned them. Philip couldn't keep from thinking, as he observed their stoic faces, that these people held his future in their hands. He was curious about them. He wondered about their families and their children and about what they had eaten for dinner at home the night before. That made it easier on him, thinking of them as if they were real people instead of players in a drama that threatened the future of everything he stood for.

At 1:45 p.m. on Friday, the jury selection was complete. Morgan's attorneys and Bennett Huff were satisfied. One of the women worked in the infants' department at Dillard's. One of the men laid telephone lines for Southwestern Bell. The jurors were ordinary people, all of them.

At 9:00 a.m. the following Monday, the trial testimony began. Philip sat silently at the defendant's table with Bennett Huff at his side, waiting for the inevitable—the parade of players, lies, unwitting pawns that had to be present for this farce to take place.

Farce was a strong word for Philip to use. But it fitted the situation. Philip marveled that a district judge the caliber of Keslow Wilson would let a case like this one go this far. Philip had seen the man in court before and knew him to be an honest, just judge.

When Morgan entered the room, Philip decided that his choice of the word *farce* had been a good one. Morgan looked beautiful. She looked innocent and pretty and pure, and for a moment he stared at her blatantly from across the room. And she stared back.

Morgan was wearing her hair down on her shoulders in a style he hadn't seen her wear since college. It had been curled on the ends, professionally he suspected. He couldn't help thinking that it wasn't the way Emily curled hers, by rolling it on heat rollers and then sitting out against the trunk of the pecan tree in the backyard reading a book until her hair set. Or chasing the girls all around the big house and tickling them and giggling and carousing until, one by one, the curlers fell out on the floor. He had stepped on one once, one day when he had visited the farm.

Morgan smiled at him once to break the stare, and then she marched to the front of the room to sit beside her lawyers. And when she spoke to one of her counsel, she reached over and laid a hand on his elbow. And Philip understood now why Bennett Huff had instructed him not to get angry with her in front of the judge or the press or the jury. He would come across as a big, bad wolf pouncing on an innocent woman. He knew, as he watched her, that was exactly what she wanted. She baited him at every turn.

Now that he knew Emily, Philip could see things he hadn't seen before when he dared to meet Morgan's eyes. There was a covered darkness in them, and he couldn't read anything there except a small light of anticipation.

As if Bennett Huff could read his mind, Philip's attorney turned his head down to the table and examined his papers once more. "That woman is going to foul up, one of these days," he whispered to his client. "There's too much malice in her to be able to cover it very long. We'll be patient."

"I'm not so sure," Philip said. "I've been waiting for a long time and it's never come."

"She's putting on a good act but she's a viper inside," Huff reassured him. "Keslow will sense that, too. And one day, I'll bet her true personality will spring out from behind her innocent disguise and bare its ugly teeth."

“Let’s just hope it’s while the jury is in the room,” Philip said.

“Yes.” Huff nodded his head in agreement. “Let’s do.”

Chapter Twelve

Philip was exhausted. If there was anything he'd come to despise, it was sitting in one place for eight hours listening to testimony about his character. If he had to hear one more person tell the court what an outstanding businessman he was, he thought he was going to slug someone.

It was an emotional and physical release for him when Bennett Huff called him, at last, to take the witness stand on his own behalf. He was certain this part would be easy. But he was wrong. Morgan Brockner knew him well enough to hurt him. She knew his weaknesses. She had spent long hours with her attorneys, briefing them, and Philip was horrified when they began firing questions at him. They asked him about the financing his father had put out for his company. They asked him about pranks he had played on fraternity brothers in college. At the end of the morning, Philip felt that the only question they hadn't asked him was his shoe size.

By noon Morgan's lawyers had painted him as an overeager businessman who was anxious to make a fast buck by doing away with his competitors. Philip could only hope that the testimony the jury heard was so contradictory that the jurors would be totally confused. That seemed like his only hope.

That, and the testimony of Clyde Robertson.

When Robertson took the stand and began telling his story, Philip wanted to jump up out of his chair and scream at the man. He lied. Blatantly. Clyde Robertson told the jury he had signed a contract with Morgan Brockner instead of Manning Commercial Real Estate and Investment, Inc. When Bennett Huff showed Clyde a copy of the contract he had signed with Manning, Clyde sadly shook his head. "I didn't sign that one," he said hesitantly. "That one must be a forgery."

As Philip considered the millions he had made for this man in his office complex transaction, he had to wonder what hold Morgan Brockner had over him. He wondered if she had paid him. But it would have had to have been an incredible sum of money to override the profits that Philip had earned him. Clyde Robertson was testifying under oath in a courtroom that he had signed a contract with her to sell his office complex. Philip was furious enough to remain stoic throughout Clyde's entire testimony. He felt as if he'd turned to stone. He couldn't move and he couldn't rationalize. If he did, he was going to hit something.

When it came Bennett Huff's turn to cross-examine the man, Philip knew his attorney was fighting for control, too. "May I ask you, Mr. Robertson, why you went ahead and accepted a $37 million sale from Philip Manning when you say you signed an exclusive contract with Morgan Brockner?"

For a split second Clyde Robertson squirmed in his seat. Then he answered Huff's question with a question. "Wouldn't you do the same thing? Would you turn down a $37 million contract when somebody offered it to you out of the blue? Of course I couldn't turn it down."

The trial continued for the remainder of the afternoon while Philip sat in a daze. Clyde Robertson's testimony made him look like a crook of the worst order.

That night, when he climbed into his car and headed home, Philip was exhausted from mentally fighting Morgan. Her lies had crushed him. He was certain he would lose the trial and possibly his company. Morgan Brockner was beating him again.

As Philip pulled his car into the parking place beside his condominium in Dallas, he faced the stairs to his front door and didn't have the gumption to climb them. He sat in the car for a while with his head propped on the steering wheel. *Father, I know this isn't what matters. Help me not to lose hope.*

The next day at the trial, Philip took his place beside his legal counsel as usual, knowing they would encounter more of the same, trying not to let his shoulders slump with weariness and defeat. Desperately, he perused Huff's notes, hoping the lawyer might have come up with something new overnight. But Bennett pursed his lips, shook his head in frustration.

Philip sensed it the moment Emily entered the courtroom. He hadn't wanted her to come. He hadn't wanted her to see this. But something made him turn and that's when he saw her, sidling into a row and finding a place to sit between a journalist from the *Dallas Morning News* and a reporter from KXAS.

The testimony began and Philip didn't know how he ought to feel about Emily hearing it. Should he feel worried that she had come? Or angry? Or glad?

Lord, help me get out of the way. Don't let anything that happens here destroy Emily's faith. In our family. In God.

But the testimony seemed designed to make her doubt everything about the Manning companies. Of course, Morgan made sure that Clint's name got brought into it, too. And, as the afternoon wore on, more details of his relationship with Morgan came to light, bleak and brutal, painting him as the businessman who would stop at nothing to punish Morgan for a relationship gone sour.

At last the judge announced a recess. Spectators rose from their seats. Several rushed to the hallway to use cell phones. Others conversed in the aisles. He tried to get to Emily in the crowd, but Huff stopped him.

"We've got to go over these notes," Bennett reminded him, catching his arm.

"In a minute," Philip said. "I've got to talk to someone."

She must have seen him glance in her direction. Emily froze, her eyes dark, her expression unfathomable. They didn't talk until they had woven through the crowd, until they had gotten close enough to speak without being overheard.

"I don't want you here," he told her.

He saw her physically flinch when he spoke.

Even so, he wouldn't back down. Philip had every intention of protecting her from this.

"You didn't...?" She struggled for words. "I'm here to support you."

"You shouldn't have come."

She had listened all morning to the sordid details of his competition with Brockner, and the stories linking his behavior to their spurned engagement. "Philip, maybe it's time you stopped telling me what I ought to do and what I ought not to do. I think we're beyond that, don't you?"

"There isn't any reason for you to be sitting here, hearing this."

Yes, he wounded her with his attempts to shove her away. "You told me you had been seeing Morgan. You never told me that things were as complicated as this."

I never wanted you to find out. But he wasn't going to make it any more complicated by apologizing for the allegations she had heard.

He could read both the doubt and the determination in her eyes. Even so, it startled him when she changed tack. "I've been praying, Philip. There is something you need to hear, and I came to say it."

As onlookers began to file back to their seats, he looked at her with all the frustration and skepticism born of these days of lies and twisted truths. "After all this, what could you have to say to me?"

"You can't let this happen." Emily's voice was quiet but it was firm. "You can't step back, it's too important to you."

"Can't you see that I don't want you to be a part of this?" he asked her.

"Go talk to Clyde, Philip. Face-to-face. Find out what Morgan has on him."

"You're asking me to face contempt of court, Emily."

"I don't think that matters in this case. I've got a feeling about this, Philip. This is the only way the truth can come out."

"Contempt of court is the last thing I need right now."

"Let Clyde see you one-on-one. Let him see what this case is doing to you."

"That's not what men do, Emily. We don't let other guys see what they're doing to us. We hide it inside."

"Bennett Huff has one more shot at Clyde on the stand tomorrow, doesn't he? God is showing me how to change, Philip. I think He can show you how to change, too."

When he walked up to Clyde Robertson's front door and knocked on it twenty minutes later,

Clyde's wife, Marsha, answered. And Philip decided she looked frightened when she saw him.

"I came to straighten out a problem, Marsha." He said it loud enough that the others in the house could hear him, too. She was holding the door against him. But Philip didn't care if she didn't invite him in. He would wait on the front porch all night if he had to.

"Let him in," Philip heard Clyde say to his wife.

Marsha swung the door open, and Philip walked into the Robertsons' front foyer. It was late, but he could see all Clyde's kids still awake in the family room. They were sitting in a row on the sofa eating popcorn and watching a movie on TV.

Clyde was ashen when he turned to his former real estate agent. "Marsha," he commanded his wife without turning to her, "get the kids in the other room."

"It's okay, Clyde." Philip saw the fear in the man's eyes and hurried to reassure him. "I'm not here to do anything irrational. I just came to find out what's going on."

Clyde Robertson glanced back over his shoulder. "Could we talk somewhere else?"

"No," Philip said firmly. "We're going to talk right here. Right now. I don't care who hears this."

"Maybe I do."

There was a guarded look in Clyde's eyes, and Philip knew immediately that the man was preparing to cover something.

"Why did you come all the way back from some exotic vacation paradise to testify against me, Robertson?" Philip's tone was coarse. Clyde's answers mattered too much now for him to be careful. He might have done the wrong thing in coming here. But he didn't think so. It was time for all of them to face reality.

"I can't talk about it, Philip." There was genuine concern in the man's eyes. "I'm sorry."

"Don't be sorry, Clyde. Be honest. Why did you come back from the Virgin Islands? Why did you tell those lies in court? You were under oath—why did you have to lie?" Again, Philip studied the man's face. "What is she paying you to testify against me?"

Robertson's eyes widened. "She isn't paying me anything." Neither man needed to mention her name. They both knew who they were talking about.

"I know how Morgan Brockner works, Clyde. I also know that you and I have had a pretty fantastic client-agent relationship. What does she have on you? Why is she making you do this?"

This time the man's face crumpled, and—no matter how uncomfortable this confrontation made

Philip—he knew the truth. *Emily was right, wasn't she, Lord? I haven't trusted You enough. I've been hiding myself.*

"No," Clyde said, but he didn't sound quite certain of his answer.

"Clyde." Philip took a step toward his client. "Give yourself more credit than this. Don't let her destroy your integrity. Once you let her beat you once, she won't back off until she's beaten you into the ground."

"She finds out a way to get to everybody, doesn't she?" Clyde asked.

"I made you a hefty profit on that business complex sale. At least tell me what I've done to deserve to lose everything."

Clyde Robertson motioned toward the den, and Philip followed him. Robertson sat on the sofa and looked up at his former agent. He was clearly a broken man. "Okay." He was staring at the floor. "I'll tell you. I'll tell you where she's got me."

"Where?"

"The office complex. When I built it, I used substandard steel beams on the foundation. I wasn't trying to rip anybody off. It was the only thing I could do at the time. But after that building sold, she sent some inspector out there and he documented the whole thing for her."

In the silence that followed, Philip could hear Clyde's children in the other room. "Who's that man, Mama? Is Daddy okay?"

"I'm an honest man. I made one wrong choice. Now she has the ammunition to ruin me."

Philip made one dry comment. "You learn not to make wrong choices when you work around Morgan Brockner."

"If Morgan releases that information about that building, I could have every lawsuit in the books slapped on me. I can't risk it, Philip."

"Oh, yes you can." Philip grasped the man by the shoulders. He was genuinely sorry for him. "You may lose face in the business community but you won't lose your own self-esteem. So you made one mistake. So what? If you let Morgan hold that over your head now, I guarantee she'll hold it over your head for as long as she lives. If we tell the truth together, it will set us both free." And Philip was thinking, *Sometimes God answers prayer not by making things go away, but by giving us the strength to get through them.*

"Those steel beams aren't a figment of Morgan's imagination," Clyde said. "If this comes out—"

"If it doesn't come out, you're going to regret it for the rest of your life," Philip said. "Think about your kids. What if they find out what you've done? Do you think they'll respect you?"

"Do you think they'll respect me if it comes out in the press that one of my buildings might not pass code? Because of my own negligence?"

"I think they'll respect you more for telling the truth, Clyde." Philip turned to go. He had done everything he could.

At eight-thirty the next morning, Emily departed the farm for Dallas District Court. She had talked to Clint and gotten permission from him to let the kids fend for themselves today. They were certainly capable of doing that.

I didn't want you here. Philip's words still resounded in her head. *You shouldn't have come.*

She would feel the pain of him pushing her away later. But for now she knew she needed to be in the city with him, where they had first met. She needed to support him, even though he had broken her heart.

Emily drove her own car to the Dallas courthouse. After she parked, she had a few minutes before the proceedings began. She strolled across the street and sat on a bench beside the old red sandstone Dallas County Courthouse. The place had long since been made into a museum with a Texas historical marker on the front door. The old building was not unlike the Ellis County Courthouse that remained in use in the town square in Waxahachie. Both buildings had been built in the mid 1890s.

It was ironic, Emily thought, that life and history had so much planned for Dallas, and this beautiful friendly old building had been outgrown a long, long time ago. Emily looked up at the old clock tower and thought of the matching one in Waxahachie that was still in use. There, the clock still bonged out the hour for the entire town to hear. The Ellis County Courthouse was still full of typing secretaries and huffing politicians stomping around on creaky floors.

It was the old building Emily gravitated to now. It was as if the past was pulling at her. But it was the pull of the past that gave Emily hope for victory in her future. The pull of the forgiveness that she could offer her mother. Because God was showing her that true forgiveness was the only way she could let go of her past. She turned away from the broken-down clock on the Dallas County clock tower and checked her wristwatch. It was time to go in. She picked her purse up off the grass and hurried across the street to the new building that housed the courts.

When she walked into the courtroom, Philip's chin was firm and his head was high and his back was set squarely against the rows of reporters watching the proceedings behind him.

Only one available seat remained, and Emily moved to take it.

Everyone around her rose when Judge Keslow Wilson entered from his chambers. The prosecution approached the bench and called its witness. Clyde Robertson. As the man took his oath for the second time, Emily could scarcely breathe. As Clyde took the steps to the stand, Emily's hands were shaking.

Please, Father. Oh, please.

And this time when Morgan's attorneys began to question Clyde Robertson, the man told an incredible story. He told the judge and the jury that he had been mistaken, that he had signed an exclusive contract with Philip Manning to sell his property. Morgan's attorneys saw what was happening and they halted the questioning immediately. But Bennett Huff had come prepared. He started asking questions where the prosecutors had left off. And then, in the middle of Clyde's testimony, Keslow Wilson stopped the proceedings.

"Are you aware," he asked Robertson, "that you were testifying under oath yesterday? Do you remember that yesterday you told a different story?"

Morgan Brockner shot out of her seat. And when Philip saw her face, he wanted to applaud.

Her demeanor had totally changed. She was no longer the demure businesswoman she had tried to portray. If she could have bared her teeth like an animal just then, she would have. "Don't do this, Robertson," she hissed.

Keslow Wilson banged his gavel against the judge's bench.

But Morgan had lost control. "You know what's going to happen to you if you back down on this story, Robertson."

"I suggest you sit down, Ms. Brockner, or I'll have you thrown out." Keslow Wilson's face was hard and unmoving.

"I suggest we take this man off the witness stand," she shrieked at the judge. "He's lying now. He's ruining everything."

"Ruining everything for whom?" Keslow Wilson asked. "For you?" The judge turned back to Clyde Robertson. "What's going on here? Why are you telling a different story today? What is this woman threatening you with?"

Morgan jumped from her chair again, but this time one of her attorneys grabbed her arm and wrenched her down beside them.

Keslow Wilson was still talking to Clyde Robertson. "Is Morgan Brockner blackmailing you, Mr. Robertson?"

Morgan's face went white. She glanced at her attorneys. Then she turned to glare at Philip.

"Tell us what's going on, Mr. Robertson," the judge said. And Bennett Huff guided the man while he told the entire story. When Clyde Robertson told the court how Morgan had threatened him, several of the jurors looked shocked. But Keslow Wilson didn't. And Philip speculated that the judge must have guessed what Morgan's involvement was in the case all along. Morgan was furious. She was sitting on her side of the courtroom glaring. But it was too late. Several reporters had already rushed from the courtroom to call in their stories. The wire services would pick it up. Emily bet it would even hit the pages of the *Wall Street Journal.*

The public would finally catch a glimpse of the real Morgan Brockner. But better than that, so would the jury. And from what they had seen, Emily didn't think they were likely to rule in her favor.

Keslow Wilson called a recess at 4:45 p.m., and then his gavel fell. Philip stood silent and still for one moment. Emily knew what he must be thinking. The battle hadn't been won yet. But it would be. Emily was sure of it.

Emily saw Philip turn, and she thought how this would have been the perfect moment to go to him. This would have been the time to let him sweep her into his arms, and she could laugh with him, as photographers were taking pictures.

This was the moment when a whole new world should have been beginning for them.

I don't want you here, Philip had said. *You shouldn't have come.* Emily darted out of the courtroom door so Philip couldn't see her, past Morgan, past the reporters, past the crowds.

Chapter Thirteen

Greg came down for breakfast shortly after Emily had left for the courthouse. He poured himself some Honey Nut Cheerios and sat and watched it sink into the milk in his bowl while he considered the things he was planning to do. Emily was going to be in Dallas with Uncle Philip all day. His father was tied up showing executive homes to a potential client from Waco. And Greg knew his sisters wouldn't tell on him. He decided it was time to put Plan B into action.

He would have gotten away without any hitch if Bethany hadn't come downstairs for breakfast to find him searching through their dad's desk for the Studebaker keys.

"What're you doing?" she signed.

"Nothing important," he told her. "Leave me alone."

"If you drive the Studebaker off the farm, Dad's going to kill you."

"I don't care," he told her. "I'm going to see Mom."

Greg and Emily had talked to Greg's father together just after the holidays, begging him to let the children see their mother. But Clint had stood by his decision not to let Greg or his sisters visit the hospital. Clint didn't want his children hurt by what their mother had become. Greg had done his best to abide by that decision. But he couldn't do that anymore, no matter how hard he tried. His father was wrong. They needed to share this together. And he felt bad for sneaking out this way. He hoped Emily would forgive him. She had tried to help him, after all, and now she was the one he was taking advantage of.

He drove the Studebaker away from the house slowly, out past the front cattle guard, and then he turned it south on the main road and headed toward town. It was almost noon when he pulled up and parked opposite the double glass doors that served as the visitors' entrance to W. C. Tenery Community Hospital.

Greg surveyed the parking lot before he climbed

out of the front seat and locked the Studebaker door. If his father arrived during this next hour and discovered what he had done, Greg knew he would probably be grounded for the rest of his life. But he didn't see a familiar car anywhere in the parking lot and he was satisfied he was safe, so he strolled into the hospital, feeling conspicuous, as if everyone there in the hallway knew who he was and why he was there.

He stopped at the information desk on the first floor and asked for directions to his mother's room. He half expected the nurses' aide behind the desk to tell him that he couldn't go in. But the girl just smiled at him. She looked younger than he was, and he thought maybe he recognized her from school. She pointed the way down the hallway to the stairs. He followed her directions and climbed the stairs and turned to his left and there it was just as she had said it would be, a hospital room with the door standing slightly ajar and a small card slipped into a metal frame that read: Amanda Manning.

Greg longed to burst through that door and pounce on his mother's bed and hug her just the same way he used to when he was a boy. But he was a young man now. And he had imagined this moment for months. She wouldn't be sleeping when he walked in. She would be sitting there, waiting for him to bound in, just the same way she had always done before, a hundred or so times, a hundred days when he had come home from school and had found her waiting for him.

"Mom?" He pushed open the door and went in.

The first thing that struck him was how tired she looked, and he felt as if he should tiptoe toward her. Even his own breathing sounded labored and heavy and loud in the room. He moved toward the bed, and he wanted to take her hand in his, but he didn't dare. He didn't know what touching her might do to her. Greg wondered if she could feel him there. "Mom," Greg said again. His own voice sounded awkward and out of place in her silent room. "How've you been?"

He didn't wait for her to answer. He knew she couldn't. He just kept talking about everything he could think of. He wanted to tell her something, anything, that would make the still form that looked like a wax image of his mother react. As he talked, he wondered what he would do if, by some miracle, she *did* move or reach for him.

"Dad doesn't know I'm here," he said to her. "We're off school for spring break. Emily—that's the lady who lives in the camp house and keeps an eye on us—well, she had to go to Dallas, so I brought the Studebaker and came on here. You should see the

Studebaker, Mom. That chrome polish you bought took all the water spots off the hubcaps."

Then he laughed. He had almost forgotten for a moment that she couldn't hear him. "Bethany borrowed some to use on her bike, but she got so much on the fenders that it took her a whole roll of paper towels to get it off. It's still smeared on there, but she rides around thinking she's hot stuff anyway."

His voice softened. He was talking about everything that came to his mind without censoring himself the way he had for months now. "Dad didn't ever want us to come. I guess he figured if he let me come, he'd have to let Bethany come, too, and seeing you like this would scare her to death. I've really wanted to spend time with you.

"Dad's tried to be strong for all of us. And he's done a good job, but he gets tired a lot and he gets mad at Lisa about something new every night. You know Lisa, always running around doing dumb stuff.

"We can't wait until you come home again, Mom. Oh, and Honey Snookems's calf is getting so big…"

Greg's voice droned on until finally, after about an hour, it faded off into silence. He sat quietly then and memorized the room where his mother had lived during the past year.

Clint had done his best to make the clinical

hospital room look homey. There were touches of the Manning family and the farm everywhere Greg looked. There was a poster that read, "Find a place you like and go there," just like the poster Lisa had given Emily. There was a hand-stitched calico pillow sewn in the shape of a sheep sitting in an old rocking chair in the corner. Greg had never seen the pillow before, but the rocker was one that had been up in the attic at the farm for ages. There was an iPod and speakers in the corner, too, one that Greg had never seen, and a bucket of *Wall Street Journals,* assorted magazines and a tattered spy novel and the Bible he remembered her carrying to church every Sunday. Greg realized that his father must be doing most of his reading aloud here early in the mornings.

On the bedside table stood an oak-framed portrait of their family together, that had been taken two summers ago; they'd been having a picnic in the pecan grove and everyone was smiling, their arms around one another. Three wooden buckets in the windows overflowed with geraniums, and Greg guessed correctly that his father had been buying blooming ones every month from the greenhouse in Waxahachie. There were personal, everyday things all around the room, too, things that belonged to his mother, things Greg realized he hadn't missed from the house—a lipstick, a white heart-shaped box of dusting powder, a pink toothbrush and a bottle of her favorite perfume.

Looking around the room like this, with his mother so still and silent in the bed, terrified him. Greg felt like he was experiencing the depth of his father's love for his mother for the first time. Visiting this room was like visiting a shrine. For the first time, Greg began to comprehend why his father had been so protective of her in this state and why he'd kept his children on the farm. Everything at home was overflowing with life...the growing things...the laughter and the arguments around the kitchen table...the kittens that were born wild and scampered in the hayloft in the barn.

When he'd heard about this place from his father, it had been so easy for Greg to imagine it that way, too, with sunlight streaming in the windows and his mother sleeping. But something much heavier than sleep hung in the room, something that had grown stronger and sadder with the passage of time. Life outside the hospital went on without his mother. Even the portrait of their family on the bedside table was already outdated. The summer before last, Bethany had been only seven. She had still been missing a front tooth when the picture had been taken. Lisa had been eleven and he had been thirteen and in the eighth grade. It seemed like a lifetime had gone by since he had been in the eighth grade. And his mom had missed it all.

Greg found himself wanting to fill her room with life, with news, with noise. He opened the blinds a little more and let the sunlight stream in across her bed. He turned on the iPod music. And even that didn't seem to be enough, so he flipped on the television, too, and got *Oprah.* The show seemed to come from another world, too, the applause, the women's voices.

He went to his mother's side and gazed down at her for a long while before he picked up her hand and squeezed it in his. He wanted to squeeze her hand hard enough so she would feel it. But she didn't move. Looking at her closely made Greg sad. She was so thin and her skin was so sallow that she looked almost transparent to him. It seemed as if he could see the sheets below her almost through her arms. "Oh, Mom," he said aloud so she could hear him over the stereo and the television set. "Hurry up and come home. We can't wait much longer."

Greg turned from her then and walked out of her room without looking back. He knew that now he would do nothing but think of her like this, lying here, silent and sallow, looking like a stranger.

And when he climbed into the Studebaker and turned the key to start the ignition, he knew he wasn't ready to face everyone at home. He needed to be alone.

He drove the Studebaker out of the hospital parking lot and found the radio station he liked. But even the rushing beat of the hip-hop music did nothing to take his pain away. He just drove around on country roads around Waxahachie for a while, thinking of everything that had happened during the past months and mostly thinking about his father. Every moment in that hospital room bore testimony to how much his dad loved his mom, how much he needed her, how much he had lost.

A familiar anger welled in Greg's throat. What right did his father have to deny the rest of them the chance to love her, to be with her, too? His mother needed them all.

"I could have been strong enough to handle it." He talked to the car, the sky, the road, the radio. "Why didn't you let me?" As he talked, his foot eased down on the accelerator. Greg felt like he was fighting against some unknown enemy. And he didn't notice it when the speedometer began creeping up and then edged on past eighty. "I could have done it. Why didn't you let any of us be there for her?" Greg let a wave of self-pity wash over him. And for one split second, and that was all, he almost wished that his mother had died. Then it would have all been over. They could have mourned and they could have told her goodbye and then his father could have let go of the searing edge of hope that was always present, always ready to tear parts of their hearts out. It would have been over. And none of them would have to be strong anymore.

How ashamed he felt, thinking of his mother's death! As long as they had any thread of hope at all, they would all cling to it. And he drove on, wondering if he should turn back toward home, letting the racing words on the radio take him away from all of it. He was in a vacuum. For a moment it was as if he didn't have a mother or a father or anyone else who could hurt him. The curve on the Maypearl road loomed up at him.

Greg had already driven this curve this morning, but he had been ready for it when he hit it. As the car went into a skid, a sharp picture came into focus in his mind. He saw his uncle Philip and Emily bending over an unmoving tiny calf lying in the dust of the corral. And his mind told him instantly what was wrong. He hadn't reacted quickly enough. And even if he had, the Studebaker was going too fast to negotiate the curve. The car veered wildly to the right and then, for one or two seconds, the vehicle itself seemed to hover in the air as if it would turn back onto the road. Then it spun onto the road shoulder and the rear tire struck a ditch, and the last thing Greg remembered was the car flipping and then all was blackness as the dust around him settled. From somewhere that seemed to be far, far away in a meadow, the hip-hop song still blared.

Members of the Ellis County Sheriff's Department traced the license plate on the Studebaker to Clint Manning only moments after two deputies arrived on the scene of the accident. The dispatcher at the Sheriff's Department in town called Clint's office but no one answered.

No one answered at Clint Manning's residence, either. Twice when she called, the telephone line was busy. The third time she called, an answering machine bleeped at her. She left a cryptic message, designed not to alarm. "Please call the Sheriff's Department. We are trying to reach you." After doing some quick research on the computer, she found that Clint Manning had a brother.

"Where is everybody?" Emily called when she arrived at the house.

"Oh, they're around," Bethany said vaguely. The girl looked worried and maybe a bit guilty. Bethany was a loving, honest person. Emily couldn't believe that the girl would be dishonest. Nevertheless, she decided to take an individual inventory of the family. "Where's Lisa?"

"In the pecan grove. She's climbing trees again. She said she'd be back at the house in a little while."

"What's Greg doing?"

Bethany hesitated for a long time before she answered. "He's with the Studebaker." And she looked like she wanted to cry. Greg had made both of his sisters promise to cover for him. Bethany thought he was doing something he needed to do. And she hadn't exactly lied to Emily. Greg *was* with the Studebaker. She just hadn't told Emily exactly where the Studebaker was.

Emily heard the confusion in Bethany's voice. She almost rephrased her question, but in the end she changed her mind. It wasn't fair to put a little sister on the spot for something her older brother might be doing. Emily made a mental note to check on Greg in the garage as soon as she got into some jeans.

Just then the phone rang. Emily hurried to answer and made a mental note that the light on the machine was flashing. Someone had already called in. "Hello?"

"I am calling to speak with Emily Lattrell," a very professional-sounding woman's voice said. "This is Sylvia Ressling, senior editor for the children's division at Hudson Publishing. We'd like to talk to you about publishing your Baby Sprout book series."

Sylvia's voice sounded so friendly, and as she began explaining her call in more detail, Emily could scarcely believe the things the editor was saying. She loved the Baby Sprout series. In her opinion, it was light, fun reading for younger readers and had a message without being preachy. She and her colleagues could see a definite slot for it in their younger children's list for the upcoming year. And they loved the illustrations. Was her illustrator a professional, she wanted to know.

Here she was on this farm in Waxahachie, Texas, floundering around in a huge sea of sudden possibilities. When she hung up the telephone, Emily felt as if a dam inside her had burst. She was a children's author, at least, she *would* be as soon as the contract was signed.

Emily picked up the phone and dialed her father's number at the bank in Decatur. Then she called Lloyd. "Holy moly," was all he could say over and over again when she told him.

She stopped her former employer by laughing

at him and asking, "Can't you say something nicer than that?"

"Of course I can. Congratulations, Emily. I'd like an autographed copy."

"You'll get one. I promise. That's easy."

After Emily hung up the telephone, she was so excited by the call that she forgot to check the other message. She sat at the kitchen table by herself and let the reality sink in. There was so much to comprehend that she couldn't do it all in one sitting. She had always dreamed of this, and now it was coming true. Her words would be distributed across the world with Philip's drawings on every page. How many children would see Baby Sprout? How many children would love him? As Emily thought about that and about the responsibilities God had seen fit to give her, it was enough to make her want to cry.

The back screen door banged open a few minutes later and the girls came inside. "Emily? What's wrong?" Lisa asked when she saw her face.

"Nothing's wrong," she answered. "Everything's wonderful." And she told them the story, signing to Bethany. Lisa hugged her so that she couldn't breathe.

"That means we have a calf with an almost-famous name," Bethany said.

Emily hadn't even considered the sudden celebrity of Honey Snookems's baby.

"I think we should celebrate," Lisa said. "What can we do? This is really exciting."

It suddenly seemed very important, sharing this time with the girls. Emily had no idea how Philip would react when he found out about this. Maybe he didn't want anything to do with it. When she'd seen him in the courtroom, it seemed he didn't want her around. He didn't want anything to do with her anymore.

But she wasn't going to let that get in the way of her relationship with the girls. Emily grabbed Lisa in one arm and Bethany in the other and squeezed them. "I'm in the mood to shop. I'll buy each of you something."

"Sounds like a good way to celebrate to me," Lisa said, grinning.

"Can I get a red Hawaiian shirt?" Bethany asked, her eyes wide. It had been ages since the sisters had been shopping together, not since before their mother had gone to the hospital.

"We'll see what we can find," Emily said.

So the three of them piled into the car and Emily drove them to the mall. They spent the next three hours having fun. If their cell phones rang, the din inside Hollister and American Eagle was too loud for them to hear a sound. They tried on outlandish fashions and added up price tags and not one of them, not Lisa or Emily or Bethany, thought about Greg or wondered where he might be.

As Philip listened to the officer on the other end of the line, his face went ashen. He was being asked to identify the driver of a 1960 Studebaker.

His voice remained steady, but Philip felt like his insides were being torn out. "That would be my nephew, Greg Manning." He almost added, *He's fifteen. Too young to have his driver's license.* But that didn't seem to really matter. What had happened to Greg? Filled with dread, he couldn't bring himself to ask the question. He only sat silently on the phone and waited for the deputy to tell him.

"We tried to locate your brother at his office and at his residence, but we couldn't find anyone. Do you have any idea where he might be?"

"No."

"Do you have a cell phone where we might reach him?"

"Of course I do." Philip recited the number. "You can get him there."

"The boy's been in an accident. We're waiting to take him to the operating room. He's bleeding internally and the E.R. doctors have already prepped him for surgery."

For once, Philip was speechless.

"If we can't get ahold of his father, are you willing, as his uncle, to take the responsibility for that decision?"

They were taking him into surgery, Philip thought, relieved. At least he was still alive.

When his phone rang again several minutes later the officer let him know that Clint hadn't answered his cell phone, either. *He must be in a meeting with clients,* Philip thought. *He's got his phone turned off so he won't be interrupted.* And suddenly, none of that seemed to matter so much anymore, not the real estate business, not important clients, none of it. He glanced at his watch. It was 2:15 p.m., and it would take him forty-five minutes to get there. "Can the doctors take my consent over the phone? I'm in Dallas. It's going to take time for me to get there."

"I'll have the surgeon call you from the hospital now," the officer confirmed. "I'll radio Dallas County and arrange for an escort. Once you get into Ellis County, you'll be fine. Our officers won't stop you, they'll know who you are."

Philip was already driving by the time the surgeon called. He gave his consent, answered questions about allergies, told them everything about Greg that he knew. He hadn't bothered to ask the surgeon the specifics of Greg's condition. Philip knew that if he had internal injuries, things were bad. And any other injuries were secondary to that. They had to find the bleeding and get it stopped.

As Philip sped south of Dallas, he was joined by a Dallas County Sheriff's vehicle with two officers inside. They led him on through the traffic and set the traveling speed at ninety miles per hour.

Once Philip crossed the county line, his escort vehicle pulled off the road and he was alone. As he thought about it, Philip was relieved he had been the first one to receive the information about Greg. It brought back so many memories of Amanda. Although Clint would have had no other choice but to approve Greg's surgery, this way his brother had not been faced with the decision. There was nothing else left to do now except get to the hospital and find Clint and Emily. And pray.

When Philip arrived at the hospital, Greg was still in surgery. Philip put several calls through to Clint, but there was still no answer. He called the house, but he only got Clint's voice on the answering machine. Because he didn't want to alarm anyone he left an intentionally vague message. And half an hour later, after Philip had taken a few minutes to stop in and see Amanda, his cell phone finally rang.

Emily and the girls had just arrived home from shopping. All their arms were full of crumpled packages, and they were all three dizzy from the lively discussion and the laughter they had shared in the car while Emily drove them home. She had been humming television-show theme songs, and the girls had been trying to guess what shows they were. And that game had degenerated further into silliness when Lisa had tried to remember all the words to the theme song for *The Flintstones.* They had all marched into the house singing, "…they're the modern stone-age fa…a…mi…ly…"

But the mood changed abruptly when Emily heard Philip's voice over the machine. She knew immediately that something was terribly wrong. At first she thought his call had something to do with the trial. But then she had a feeling that wasn't why he'd called. Was it the hospital? Immediately, she thought of Amanda. She had gotten the message from the Sheriff's Department, too.

"Philip?" she asked, and she was suddenly even more frightened, just hearing his voice. Emily thought Amanda had died.

"Philip? It's me. What's wrong?"

"Are you home? Where's Clint? He hasn't been in his office all afternoon."

"He had meetings. And he's been showing property."

"Do you know what he's showing? Can you find him for me?"

"I can try. I'll get Greg, too. We'll split the territory."

"Emily…"

"Greg must still be working on the Studebaker in the garage. I think he's got a crush on his car. I feel sorry for any girl who falls in love with him."

"Em. Stop."

"The poor girl doesn't stand a chance with all the competition she'll get from that Studebaker."

"Emily." Philip's voice was husky. He hated to tell her this. She hadn't even missed Greg yet. And she was his adopted mother. He already knew she was going to hold herself responsible for what had happened.

She finally stopped jabbering long enough to realize he was trying to tell her something. She waited, finally giving him the chance.

"Greg's here. In the hospital." How badly Philip wanted to say, *Greg's here with me.* That would have made receiving this news easier for her. But he couldn't hedge the truth. Greg wasn't with him.

Greg was in surgery. He had been on the operating table for two hours.

"What's he doing there? Did you come by and pick him up?"

If Emily had been watching Bethany's face just then, if she had seen how closely the girl was watching her lips, she would also have seen the girl go pale.

"He's in surgery. He's had a car accident."

"No!" Emily had shirked her duties to the children because of the trial. And she had been so excited about the telephone call from Hudson Publishing in New York City that she had forgotten to even check on the teenager. "I'm coming now. I'm bringing the girls with me. And I'll find Clint on the way."

She hung up and turned toward the girls. She didn't have to say anything to them. They had heard enough to understand that the situation was grave. They threw their new clothes on the kitchen table and the three of them ran back to the car. This time, there was no singing as they drove toward town.

They found Clint showing a property to his client at the second executive home they drove by. Emily jumped out of the car and ran to him. "Clint, your phone's turned off!" She grasped his arm and spoke to him in a hushed voice. He turned to his clients, a man and his wife, and his face was gray but his voice was composed.

"I have an emergency with my son," he told them. "Let me get a colleague to continue showing you these homes." Then he followed Emily and the girls in his own car and they all just managed to keep to the speed limit. At the hospital, they walked into the lobby and went upstairs to the surgery waiting room without having to ask anyone where to go. They didn't have to. They followed Clint, who had done this once before.

Clint was clutching Bethany in his arms when they reached the top of the stairs, and Lisa was clinging to Emily. When Philip saw all of them, he had never been so glad to see anyone in his life. He had taken the responsibility for Greg's surgery because no one else could be reached, and the decision was starting to weigh on him. He spoke to all of them quietly, even the girls, and told them that he had given the doctors his permission to operate. Clint sank into a chair and buried his face in his hands just as the surgeon came through the operating-room door.

"Are you Greg's father?" The doctor reached out his hand to Clint. He already knew who Philip was. He knew about Amanda, too. Everyone at the hospital did. And he had assisted on her surgery a year ago, too. One couldn't easily forget a case like that.

As the doctor continued speaking, his voice was warm and kind and full of relief. "Your son is going to be fine. We got him mended easily, once we found out where the problem lay. He's got a broken leg and three broken ribs and a punctured stomach, so it'll take a while for him to get back on his feet. But he's in recovery now, and I've listed his condition as stable. You can see him in a little while, after the anesthetic wears off."

Philip flinched visibly. *Greg was still unconscious.* But the doctor hadn't seen anything unusual during the surgery. And Greg was young and strong. He couldn't end up like his mother, Philip reasoned. Clint hugged both his girls to him and rocked them slightly as Emily stood beside them. For a moment Philip felt like an outsider. Of all the family in the room, he wouldn't release himself and surrender to his feelings. Instead he looked up at Emily who was standing there, pale and steadfast beside his brother and his nieces.

It was after six in the evening when Clint glanced at his watch and suggested they go downstairs for a bite to eat in the cafeteria. The girls were both tired and hungry, and Greg wasn't out of recovery yet, so when they left, the physician on duty promised to send a nurse downstairs to find them if the boy started to awaken.

Philip was the only one who didn't want to leave the waiting room, but Emily convinced him to come, too. Together, they began to piece together the events of Greg's day. Emily remembered the comment Bethany had made this morning. "He's with the Studebaker." She turned to the girl and signed gently to her.

Bethany told them everything they needed to know. "He came to the hospital. He said he was coming to visit Mom."

"What?" Clint slammed his fist on the Formica table, spilling his coffee out of the cup into the saucer. "What did he mean by doing that without my permission?"

Bethany began to cry at Clint's reaction, and Lisa bent forward to hug her little sister. Even Emily was alarmed at his rage. "Clint, I'm sorry," she said.

Philip's hand shot across the table and grasped her arm. "Don't you dare apologize." He knew there was a chain of circumstances that brought Greg to the hospital, first as a visitor and now as a patient. He wouldn't let Emily distance herself from this family. He wouldn't let his brother burden anyone else with his guilt. If Greg rebelled, it was all Clint's fault. And Philip was desperate to keep Emily from taking it upon herself. With his grip, he made her look at him. "Don't blame yourself for what happened to Greg. Don't you dare do that."

"He was driving around the county like a maniac," Clint said, his head in his hands. "I never wanted any of you kids to see her." Emily knew he had wanted to protect them from some horrible injustice and pain. It was the same thing Greg had realized earlier as he'd stood in Amanda's room and noticed the homey things his father had gathered for her. Clint had wanted to carry the weight of the world on his own shoulders. He didn't want the consequences of all that hurt to rest on the shoulders of the people he cared about, too.

"I've figured out what you've been trying to do, Clint. And it's admirable. All this time I've been thinking you were being hard-hearted to the kids."

"How dare you tell me how to raise my own children," Clint said, his voice breaking under the strain. "I never asked for your opinion."

"Sure, it came across as if you were trying to protect them. But it came across as more than that, too. Maybe you didn't think they were strong enough to handle this. Or maybe you thought you could keep Amanda closer to you by not sharing your grief with the kids."

"Philip," Clint said. "This isn't the time."

"When is the time going to be?" Philip asked his brother. "You know each one of them, even Bethany—" he glanced at his niece "—every one of them is strong enough to handle this. But you love these crazy kids so much that you don't want them to have to feel the same things that you feel. You're doing your darndest to feel everything for them."

That was the minute Philip's head began roaring. *And aren't you doing the same thing, too? Isn't that the same thing you did when you told Emily you didn't want her at the trial? You were trying to protect her from all of it. You were trying to protect the woman you love.*

Philip couldn't have stopped, even if he'd wanted to. And now he knew that the words he said to his brother were words he needed to hear, too.

Emily, he thought. *Can you ever forgive me? I've done the same thing to you that makes me so angry at my brother.*

Lord, how easy it is to see faults in others when we can't see them in ourselves.

Like Clint, I tried to protect someone. I tried to protect Emily. He said that he didn't want her at the trial. But that was the wrong thing to do.

"You're denying them a part of themselves, Clint. You're denying them their grief and their hope. And, in the end, you might be denying them their chance to a front-row seat to a miracle."

You can't protect each other from hurt, no matter how much you want to. God often calls us to go through something instead of going around it.

Silence.

"Right now, Clint, you're trying to play the game as if this never happened, as if she was never gone. But she is gone, bud. And if these kids don't truly realize that fact, if you don't let them feel the grief, then they won't get to feel the hope and the wonder if she gets better, either."

Philip saw his brother watching his two children whom he loved more than anything in the world with tears in his eyes, and thinking about the third, his firstborn son, lying upstairs in the recovery room. Philip could see that his brother realized the words were right, that he owed all three of his children much more than what he had been able to give them on his own.

Silently, Clint stood and extended both hands to them, one to each of his daughters.

"Come on," he said to them. "It's time we went to see your mother."

It was Lisa who understood the complete significance of this moment more than Bethany. Their father had decided it was time to share something important with them. She still had hold of her little sister's hand. The three of them formed a small, simple semicircle as they left the table in the cafeteria and went to retrieve something that the three of them had lost a long, long time before.

Chapter Fourteen

Greg was weak but feeling fine when the doctors authorized a move to a private room for him.

"How are you feeling, son?" Clint asked.

"I'm okay, Dad." Greg glanced at the broken leg ruefully. "This cast rocks. I'll have to get every girl in the school to autograph it for me."

"I'm sure your sisters will oblige," Clint teased. "I don't know about the rest of the girls in Waxahachie."

"I intend to make this worth the hassle. I'll bet this thing drives me nuts when it starts itching. The least I can do is get some good out of it."

"Sounds like a plan to me."

When a nurse came in to bring Greg's medication, she helped him move to a wheelchair. She was blond and pretty and Greg was willing to bet that she was just out of college. "Will you autograph my cast?"

"Certainly," she said, obliging him, and Greg winked at his father across the room.

Greg looked at the nurse seriously then. "It feels good to be up for a while. Would it be okay if I took this chair and my dad and I went for a walk?"

"It wouldn't hurt," she told him. "Your father can push you. But don't go far."

Greg turned and looked at his father. "Can we visit Mom's room?"

Clint's face darkened. But he didn't say no. He stood from where he was sitting and pushed his son down the hall.

"Thank you, Dad."

"Your sisters have both been in to see her, too," Clint said.

"How did they do?"

"Fine," Clint told Greg. "It didn't upset them as much as I'd thought it would." Clint pulled open the door and pushed his son's wheelchair inside.

"See." Greg craned his neck and looked up at his father. "Dad, you can always depend on us kids."

"Right." Clint glanced pointedly at his son's cast. "Sometimes I can depend on you to be real dumb."

"Did I mess up the Studebaker real bad?"

"The frame's bent, son," Clint answered him. "I don't know if it can be restored or not."

"Dad, I'm really sorry."

Neither of them noticed the slight movement in the bed beside them. They were both too intent on the things they had to say to each other.

"I need to apologize, too, son," Clint said. "That's one reason I went ahead and brought the girls up to see your mother. Your uncle Philip made me realize…" His voice trailed off.

"Hey." The weak comment came from the bed to their left. Amanda's voice was sluggish but no more so than if she had only been awakened from a heavy sleep after twelve hours…twelve hours, instead of twelve months. "If you two are going to have one of these deep discussions, why don't you both go downstairs? I'm tired. I've had a hard day. Bethany…" What had Bethany done today? she asked herself. She couldn't quite remember.

At Amanda's words, her open eyes, Clint and Greg were almost too stunned to move. Almost. Their eyes locked and the color drained from Clint's face. Everything seemed to be happening in slow motion, as if every second might be an eternity and every movement had been choreographed as a freeze-frame pantomime. Clint went to his wife's side. And Greg tried to move the wheelchair forward without much success. Greg felt like a chair with four legs that hadn't been glued together yet. All the parts he needed to move together to get to his mother's bedside were going in opposite directions. And then, when he finally gave up his struggle and sat long enough for the truth to sink in, he realized what this was going to mean to all of them. His mother had come back.

Amanda was staring up at the ceiling thinking it looked odd. She was thinking that the ceiling was unfamiliar, all bumpy, with sparkly things in it, and that it was strange because a minute ago she had awakened and had heard Clint and Greg talking and she'd thought she was at home in their bed, with a fire in the fireplace, waiting for Clint to come climb in beside her and hold her. But now she remembered she was in the hospital.

"Clint?" She turned to her husband and grasped his hand. Then she saw her son sitting in the wheelchair across the room. "Greg? What did you do to your leg?"

"I broke it."

Clint's words were slow and deliberate, so as not to frighten her. He addressed his son without once letting his eyes waver from his wife's. "Greg? Why don't I push you outside and we'll let somebody important out there know what's going on in here?" He didn't want to say doctors or nurses. He had no idea if Amanda could remember anything. And he wondered if she even knew where she was.

Maybe give us another few days and none of us will be worried about doctors or nurses, he thought. Doctors or nurses. It seemed to Clint that doctors and nurses had been ruling all their lives forever.

"Manderly." He stroked her arm as he spoke to her. He didn't know how much he should tell her, how much she was capable of comprehending. "Before I go outside, try to remember something for me, will you? Do you remember getting ready to come to the hospital? For surgery?"

"That's right." Amanda looked pleased. She had checked in yesterday morning—or had it been this morning—for gynecological surgery. Slowly she raised her torso and swiveled her hips beneath the blankets. "It must have gone pretty well." Her eyes were wide. Maybe the local anesthetic just hadn't worn off yet. "I'm stiff but I certainly don't feel an incision. When do I get to go home? How's everything at the farm? I'm ready to get out of here."

"What is this?" Clint smiled down at her. "You sound just like your son. Why does everybody want to go home?"

"Because we like it there," she told him, winking at Greg. And Clint just stared down at her. She was glad to see him, too, but she couldn't understand why he was looking at her that way. She had just gone in to have a simple cyst removed yesterday. The doctors had told her there was nothing she should worry about. And now Clint was hovering over her, looking as if a miracle had happened because she was awake and speaking to him. And there was Greg, sitting in a wheelchair.

She remembered something then, about the meals she prepared for them before she left for the hospital. "How were those chicken enchiladas? I tried one of Mom's recipes. Did y'all like them?"

Clint was smiling at her now, and she didn't understand the gleam in his eyes. "They were wonderful." He couldn't even remember them.

"Greg? What happened?" Clint was laughing now, laughing at life and at miracles and at her menu. How could they have possibly survived for twelve months on one pot roast and a pan of chicken enchiladas?

Father, You are good. Oh, Father. Thank You.

He bent over her and stroked her hair. But she wasn't amused. She wanted to know why he was laughing at her. But when he moved back, she saw that there were tears in his eyes and Greg's, too, great pools of them glittering there, and she reached up and kissed Clint's hand even though she didn't understand why it was that he was crying.

Chapter Fifteen

Philip ran his eyes down the list he had made.

(1) Mow lawn.

(2) Trim grape arbor.

(3) Paint fence.

It was an odd list. If anybody back at the office were to see this, they would laugh. But as Philip ran his eyes down it once more, he decided that it was probably the most important list he had ever made. These were things Clint had asked him to do at the farm before Amanda arrived home.

Clint was spending his every waking minute at the hospital with his wife. The doctors were observing her carefully. All indications were that she would be coming home within the week. Clint wanted everything to be perfect for her.

The entire family had started to make ready for her arrival. Greg was home now and was mending nicely. Even though the doctors had told him to rest, he had spent time in his closet straightening his clothes and organizing his sports paraphernalia on the shelves. When Emily had found him in his room working, she had ordered him back to bed, all the time clucking at him like an enraged mother hen. Even now, Emily was taking so much responsibility for them. She wanted things to be perfect for Amanda almost as much as Clint did. Emily was outside now, washing windows. He could hear her scrubbing on the panes outside Clint's study.

Philip rose from the sofa and went into the room so that he could watch her working. She was outside polishing the glass with ammonia water and old newspapers. Her hair was tied away from her face with a faded navy-blue and white bandanna, and she was so intent on her work that she didn't see him enter the room. Philip watched her while she stepped back from the window and frowned up at a smudge she had missed on the left-hand side.

Would she ever forgive him for pushing her away? Would she be able to understand that he knew now how wrong he'd been for not wanting her there? Soon Emily wouldn't be a mother for the children anymore. He wondered if that made her feel sad, unneeded. Philip had seen what a strong woman she could be. He knew that in spite of mixed emotions she would be happy for them.

"Need help washing?" he asked through the glass.

She shook her head at him, and he leaned his forehead against the window.

"Don't!" she shrieked as she waved one of her cleaning rags at him. "You're smearing it!"

He touched the glass with one finger and she gave him a disgusted look. "I'm coming out there."

When Philip stepped out onto the porch, he squinted his eyes into the sun so he could see the approaching car. He had no idea who this could be. It certainly wasn't his brother.

When the woman opened the door on the driver's side and climbed out, Emily gasped. "Mother?"

"I wanted to see you." The woman's voice was soft. "It's been a long time."

The stricken-looking older woman stared at Emily. Emily asked, "What are you doing here?"

"Darling, hello."

For an instant Emily felt totally lost. She wheeled around to find Philip, and there he was, supporting her. No matter how he had hurt her, Emily was glad to have him here now. And suddenly, as she stared at her mother, she thought what a miracle it was, that here were the three of them, standing together on a gravel driveway, when they'd been estranged for so long. It was a beginning of sorts to her, just realizing that loving them was worth the pain.

"Hello, Mother."

"Have I shocked you? I'm sorry." The woman clenched her coat against her chest. "I wanted to see my daughter. I've missed you."

"I've missed you, too." Emily had been missing her mother for a very long time.

"Your father told me what happened with your book. He tells me you're having it published."

"You've talked to Daddy?" Emily asked.

"Last week." The woman paused. Her eyes were full of pride. "He told me all about it. It makes me very proud of you."

"Thank you." Emily was still confused. She didn't know why her mother had come.

"Are you going to write several of them?"

"I'd like to." Emily paused.

"Are you going to quit your job on the farm because of this?"

For a moment Emily tried to hear dissatisfaction in her mother's words, tried to imagine her mother finding fault again because of what Emily had sacrificed to come to the farm. But a nudge in her heart told her this wasn't the case.

"My job here on the farm is over. I'm leaving, but not because I sold my book." Emily chose her words carefully. She had almost finished her responsibilities here. She was proud of what she'd been able to do, but leaving the farm would be painful. "The children's mother is coming home soon. Then they won't need me anymore." Emily braced herself again for a reprimand. She was certain her mother would find something unsatisfactory with the situation.

"I can see why you like it here. It's beautiful."

"Yes. It is."

Emily studied her mother. Something seemed subtly different about her. Her mother's face, although devoid of color, pale and powdery, looked happy.

When Emily's mother smiled like this, she resembled a stranger. She looked beautiful. But she looked worried, too. She didn't want her daughter to know how frightened she had been of this visit. But her counselor had told her it was something she needed to do. It had taken every ounce of her strength to go to her husband and tell him what she needed to say. And now she needed to go to her daughter, too.

"I'm headed out of town on a trip, going out to the mountains with a few of my friends. To Jackson Hole. It's a victory celebration of sorts."

"Friends?" Emily still held the polishing rag at her side, but she had long forgotten it, Philip could tell.

"I'm working at a flower shop in Garland now. I've made a few friends since I got out of rehab. And I invited your father. He's going, too."

Emily didn't know which question to ask first. "Daddy's going?" Then, "Rehab?"

"Yes, Emily." Although the woman's voice was soft, that didn't keep her pride from coming through as she spoke. "I've tried so many times, even when you were young, and I never was able to make it work. I didn't want to disappoint you again."

Emily scarcely dared look up at her mother for fear she might be mistaken.

Her mother prodded her. "I *did* disappoint you, didn't I?"

Emily nodded. "Yes. You did."

The woman took a step toward her daughter. "You don't need to give me an answer now. That isn't what I've come for. But I didn't want to leave on my trip without asking for you to forgive me. While I'm gone, I'd like you to think of that."

Emily's mother didn't dare tell her daughter that she had called the treatment center the afternoon Emily had phoned to thank her for the journal. She didn't quite know how to tell her daughter what an impact the few words of thanks had for her. She only wanted Emily to know that she had done it. "I'm completely sober. I've been sober for three months, thirteen weeks and four days. I still have a long way to go."

"Mama?" And when she said it, Philip thought Emily sounded like the little girl she had never been given the chance to be.

"Yes?"

"You said Daddy was going with you on this trip?"

"I did."

"I…I don't understand."

"I've had this same conversation with him. I've found a church I really like. With God's help, I've been able to stick to a program this time. And your father and I have decided we'd like to see what might be…salvaged."

Emily swiped the bandanna off her head without even thinking. She squeezed it in both fists with raw emotion.

"Our marriage didn't stand a chance. None of our relationships did."

"Oh, Mama." Still, Emily didn't move toward her.

"There are a great many things I've been wanting to tell you." Emily's mother's voice was quavering now. "I realize there are big chunks of your childhood that I don't remember. I only wish…"

She started to say, *I wish I could bring some of those years back.* But that wasn't what was important to her any longer. She knew she had no right to the past. But she had a right to everything that would be happening now.

"You're taking responsibility for that?" Emily interrupted her mother. She could scarcely believe what was happening. She had yearned to hear these words for so long. There was a rush of happiness from somewhere deep within her. "But I take responsibility for it, too. I always knew that I did something to you. I always knew that there was some reason you weren't proud of me."

"You blamed yourself."

"Who else could I blame? I blamed God. Most of all, I blamed myself."

"Sweetheart." When her mother finally took her hand, Emily didn't flinch or pull away. "I love you."

Emily's voice bleated, "You do?"

An awkward, prolonged silence hung between them for a moment. Neither knew what to say next. A great wall had come tumbling down between them, but neither knew how to deal with the open space.

"I'm so sorry. So sorry that you never knew I loved you. Sorry I wasn't there for you."

Emily knew then that, during all those years,

this was the moment the Heavenly Father had been preparing her for.

"Thank you for praying for me, Emily," her mother said. "All those years. You prayed for me until you had nothing left to do but give up."

"I shouldn't have given up," Emily said.

Her mother said, "I believe God is answering all those prayers for you. Even now."

There is nothing stronger than the prayer of a child.

The woman didn't say anything more to her daughter. She only held her arms out to her.

Emily reached out to her mother and hugged her close. Then Emily stepped back and stared at her. There were a thousand things she wanted to say to her mother, but only one thing really mattered. "I do forgive you, Mother." She paused. "And you need to forgive me, too, Mama. For giving up." For the first time a voice sang in her heart, and she could see this, too. "Maybe your drinking made me feel like you didn't care about me, that you were ashamed of me, all that time, and my anger and hurt were making you feel the same way."

This time, it was her mother's turn to remain silent. Then, "I'd better go. I have a plane to catch. Can we talk more after your dad and I come home?"

Emily nodded. She said nothing more. She just stood by the house and watched her mother go. As the car drove away, Philip saw her lean against the window she hadn't wanted him to smudge and let her breath out in a rush. For the first time since she'd been a little girl, she had a family of her own, too. As the car disappeared along Maypearl Road, her tears of victory, genuine and precious and well fought for, began to slip down her cheeks in earnest.

There were many subtle changes around the farm now that Amanda was coming home. Emily and the girls had washed windows and ironed curtains until Emily thought her arms would break. The geraniums were back in their places on the balcony and the railing had been painted with a fresh coat of white. The bed in Clint's room upstairs was covered with clean sheets and a fresh quilt. The girls had been out all morning picking wildflowers in the meadow, and they were everywhere now, in huge weedy clusters. They made the whole house smell fragrant and fresh.

Emily straightened her back and looked around the front room for the last time. This place was so beautiful, and it had come to be such a special home for her. But now it was time for her to go to another home, to the place where she had belonged before she had come here. This was going to be Amanda's home again. The children didn't need an Absolutely Mom any longer.

Emily thought, as she looked around, that nothing could ever really stay the same. And it struck her how much her own life was changing, too. This was the part of being an adopted mother Abbie Carson had told her about months ago…the part where Amanda Manning came home to her family…the part where Emily would be asked to leave. This was the part where she would have to learn her hardest lesson about love. This was the part where she would have to learn how to let it go.

Emily thought of her mother and her father. Her own family might be scattered and hurting and fighting to heal. But she had learned something about them from caring for the Mannings. Clint and Amanda had fought to love one another no matter what the cost. They had proved to her that love could last. The Mannings didn't flit around in the middle of a crisis banging into one another and knocking one another off course. They held together and they trusted one another and they held on tightly to the things that really mattered.

"Whoa…Mama… Easy…" Emily heard Philip's voice out in the front yard and she turned to gaze out the window at him. She saw him running across the front yard chasing Honey Snookems and her calf. The girls had decided Honey needed to be waiting in the front yard when their mother arrived, so Philip had agreed to do the cattle herding this morning. At the sight of Philip, her heart twisted. He had been such a good uncle to the kids. She had fallen in love with him here, where he belonged, herding cows and growling up into trees. Philip had given his brother so much. He had been through so much himself, with winning the trial and fighting Morgan and everything else he had to stand up for.

I don't want you here, he had said. After the trial, both of them had been so busy helping Greg heal and getting ready for Amanda to come home, they had never gotten the chance to discuss what he meant by those words.

And, although Philip hadn't taken the chance to say the rest of it, she knew she could finish his thought without ever hearing it.

I don't want you in my life.

Emily shut her eyes to squeeze back her tears. How she was going to miss being a part of Philip's life, a part of the Manning clan.

"I'm turning them over to you now, Amanda,"

she whispered to the sky. "Take good care of them for me."

As if on cue, Emily heard Clint's car turn off the roadway and cross the cattle guard.

"They're here!" one of the girls shrieked from upstairs. Emily gripped the windowsill as two pairs of legs pounded down the stairs. Greg was outside already, waiting on the front porch in his wheelchair. Philip stopped chasing Honey and he stood by the cow while Clint drove the car up and parked it as close as he could to the front sidewalk. Philip hurried toward the car and opened the door on the passenger side. Then he reached into the backseat and pulled out Amanda's suitcase.

As Emily watched him, it struck her what an important part of this homecoming Philip was. As they all stood together in the driveway hugging, Emily wanted to freeze the scene as if on film and hold the picture in her mind forever.

Everyone walked toward the house together, and Clint helped Amanda along with one arm around her waist. As the front screen door swung open, Emily felt that perhaps she should run away. But the dark-headed, frail beauty who walked in the front door stopped her. "You're Emily." Amanda's voice was soft and melodic. Emily was entranced by it.

"Hello, Amanda." She stood before the woman

who was a stranger to her yet not a stranger, too. Then she hugged her.

Amanda looked at the petite, spunky blond woman who was standing in her living room and felt a strange kinship with her. This was Emily, the Emily who had run her household for months while she had been sleeping. At first, when Amanda had found out about Emily, she had almost been jealous. Emily had shared a part of her family's lifetime that she would never be able to share. But as the days had worn on and the children and Clint had told her stories about Emily, Amanda began to feel as if they knew each other well, as if they had somehow talked. And perhaps they had, in Emily's dreams and prayers.

"A woman's family is the most precious thing she can lay claim to," Amanda said to her. "Thank you for taking care of mine."

"You're welcome," Emily almost whispered. "Thank you for sharing them with me. I've grown to love them all." She had to choke back her tears then. "It's going to be very hard not to be a part of this family any longer."

Clint wrapped his arm around Amanda's waist. She was still weak, and it was time to help her upstairs to her room. As Emily watched the two of them climbing the stairs together, she suddenly felt very alone. The tears poured down her face, and she made no attempt to hide them anymore.

As she cried silently, Emily felt a strong arm slip around her waist.

Philip.

Emily flinched at his touch. She didn't dare look up at him.

"I'm being so selfish, I know," she said. "I'm so happy that Amanda's home. It's just hard for me to let go of them. They've become my family, too."

For a long time Philip didn't speak. She hadn't expected him to. From upstairs she could hear the sounds of the family getting their mother settled in.

"I'd better go to the cabin and finish loading the car. Time to get on the road, to get back to my place in the city."

"Emily." Philip's voice was grim. "We have to talk."

"No, we don't," she told him. "You don't have to say any more."

"Yes, I do." He grabbed her arm, wouldn't let her move. "You heard all those things I said to Clint the other day."

"When?"

"When Greg finally went to the hospital to see his mother."

Emily's shoulders slumped. She didn't see what that had to do with her.

"All those things I said to Clint. About how unfair it was to protect his son from life. I understood his motives, Emily. He was doing the wrong thing for the right reasons. He wanted to protect the kids because of how much he loved them. I realized I was doing the same thing to you."

"What?"

"At the trial. When I told you I didn't want you there, listening to everything Morgan had to say. Your newfound faith is amazing. I didn't want to jeopardize that, no matter what. I didn't want something else to come along and steal it. Because I love you so much."

"Philip?"

"I couldn't bear to think of that happening to you."

"What do you mean?"

"There was a time in my life after Morgan when I decided that God never intended for me to fall in love again. I decided that God had called for me to live my life as a single man. But, Emily, I don't think so anymore."

"I know that," she whispered. She and Philip still had so much to share. He was already working on several new sketches for Baby Sprout and Priscilla. But Emily knew it wouldn't be the same any longer.

It couldn't be. She didn't belong here the way she once had, when they'd first worked on the book.

"I wonder..." Philip stopped talking and grinned mysteriously.

"What?" she asked him. "What are you wondering?"

"I wonder whether this little creation of ours will have your hair or my hair," Philip commented flippantly. "It could be either, you know."

Emily shot him a smile. "Guess that's up to the artist. Baby Sprout doesn't have my hair. And I don't think you gave him yours."

Philip chuckled. He could see she still didn't comprehend what he was trying to tell her. He looked at Emily, and the love he felt for her welled up within him.

"For heaven's sake," he said nonchalantly as he traced the tip of her nose with his finger. "I hope his hair isn't gray. Wouldn't he be an abnormal baby if he was born with gray hair?"

"A baby?" Emily was still confused.

"Our baby." Philip's voice was soft now. "I'm not talking about Baby Sprout, Emily, I'm talking about the other work you and I have left to do. I'm talking about building a family together."

Emily lifted her face to his in wonder.

He cupped her chin in his hand. "I want you to

marry me, Emily." Philip's voice was thick with conviction. "I want you to stay a part of this family forever."

She was crying again now, and she stretched her arms up to his face and pulled him down to kiss her. Afterward, she looked at him as he stood above her, so solid, so steadfast, and she knew this man, and her faith in God, was all she would ever need. And she was willing to make a commitment to him. She was willing to fight to make that love last a lifetime. And she knew now, as she gazed up at the man who loved her, that the Heavenly Father had always been watching over her in her life, listening, hearing her prayers, caring for her. He was a God with a personal, intimate interest in her life from the very beginning.

She almost thought she could hear Him say, *If I could have sent my son to die for only one person, only you, I would have done it. I love you that much.*

Only you.

"Yes." Emily nodded her head at Philip as all the things she felt for this man poured forth from her eyes. "I love you, Philip, and I want to be your wife more than anything in the world."

Philip bent to kiss her, and when he did, Emily reveled in the sensation of his embrace. She felt totally protected, totally anchored to the man who had come to mean everything to her. She felt totally anchored to the God who ruled her life. And as the two of them clung together in the middle of a place that had become a home of sorts to both of them, they felt, at last, the warmth, the all-encompassing peace that comes from having faith in God and in each other.

QUESTIONS FOR DISCUSSION

1. Talk about Philip's reaction to Morgan Brockner. As followers of Christ, what should our response be to people who betray us, mistreat us and lie to us? How do you reconcile "Love your enemies" (Luke 6:27) with "be shrewd as serpents, and innocent as doves" (Matt 10:16)?

2. Emily had established herself in her career before she gave it up to work for Absolutely Moms. Philip had built a successful real estate business and nearly lost it all. Discuss the idea of pursuing personal goals with relinquishing every aspect of our lives to Christ. Can you do both at the same time? Could the pursuit of our goals cause us to miss God's best for us?

3. "And Emily found a strength in Philip, a strength that she didn't have, because he was able to talk about things that mattered to him." (p. 63) Describe that strength in vulnerability. How does that apply to honesty in fellowship? Discuss how finding your identity solely in Christ could allow you to be more open in relationships.

4. Emily said to her mother, "I'm not being disrespectful. I'm telling you something you need to know." (p. 151) Repeatedly in the story the characters are forced to tell each other things that might be hard to hear. Too often Believers equate being "nice" with being loving. Talk about situations where saying the hard thing to someone might not seem "nice," but may actually be the loving and right thing to do.

5. Emily's Baby Sprout story reflects her own heart's desires. If you were to write a children's book, what would the story be? How would it reveal your own "mythical autobiography"? In what ways would it reflect God's imprint on you?

6. Emily described an Absolutely Mom as a "woman who had nothing left to prove professionally…a woman who trusted something beyond herself, to guide her into touching someone else's life." (p. 104) How can you emulate that creed in your life whether you are a mom or not? What is that "Something" that can always be trusted?

7. Emily's childhood disappointments squelched her young faith. Talking about her mom, Emi-

ly said, "I prayed so many times for God to fix her, to make her be well, but he never helped her. Why should I trust a God like that?" (p. 167) How do you think Emily would describe her journey back to faith? Where are you in your faith in Christ? If He has brought you through a period of doubts, share what led you back to Him. During the hard times, where do you think God was?

8. When Emily found Lisa in the pecan tree, she didn't want to tell her things like "everything happened for a reason." (p. 79) If Emily had the faith then that she had at the end of the story, what do you think she would have wanted to say to Lisa? What would you say to someone in Lisa's situation? What would be a comfort to you?

9. Read Proverbs 17:22. In light of this verse, what do you think of Amanda's advice to Lisa, "As long as I could find something to laugh about, I could face just about anything that went wrong." (p. 78)

10. Clint tried to protect his kids from their mom's condition. Philip tried to protect Emily from

the details of the trial. Are you trying to protect anyone from something difficult? Why do you think we do that? Can you think of a situation where that kind of protection would be the best reaction?

11. How did Emily come to a place where she could forgive her mother? Do you consider forgiveness a process or a decision? Do you think it is possible to forgive even if the offender never asks for forgiveness? Why or why not? Is it possible to forgive without Christ?

12. In *The Christian's Secret of a Happy Life,* Hannah Whitall Smith said, "that man's part is to trust, and God's part is to work." (p. 28) Discuss this idea from the perspective of each of the main characters. How does this apply to your life? Does it make you feel free or out of control?